A WINTER MIRACLE
A FOUR SEASONS NOVELLA

NICKY PRIEST

OTHER BOOKS BY NICKY PRIEST

The Heartland Series

Heart & Soul

Mind & Soul

Jason Harper Series

Perception

The Miller Family Series

Unholy Trinity

Unholy Desires

Unholy Fears

Unholy Passion

Standalone Novels

Somewhere Love Remains

Takes You

One Night

Standalone Novellas

Chase the Knight

A Winter Miracle

Copyright © Nicky Priest 2019

Cover Illustration by Francessca Wingfield

Editor: Stephanie Farrant at Farrant Editing

All rights reserved. No part of this book may be reproduced or transmitted in any form or by any means, electronic or mechanical, including photocopying, recording, or by any information storage and retrieval system, without written permission from the author, except for the inclusion of brief quotations in a review.

This book is a work of fiction. Names, characters, businesses, places, events and incidents are either the products of the author's imagination or used in a fictitious manner. Any resemblance to actual persons, living or dead, or actual events is purely coincidental.

ACKNOWLEDGMENTS

As usual, I never know what to right here, so I shall keep it simple.

To everyone who encouraged me and told me I could get this book written for Christmas 2019, when I didn't believe I could.

Thank you.

Thank you for believing in me and my ability to get this book finished and out there for everyone to enjoy.

This one is for all of you

PROLOGUE

MUM: *Check.*
Dad: *Check.*
Andy: *Check.*
Bobby: *Check*, *check* and triple *check*.

She couldn't quite believe it. Even though she had left it until the last minute, she had finally finished her Christmas shopping. She'd been putting it off for weeks, not to mention she had been so busy at work. There was nothing new about that, but it was always busier this time of year. She had never left her shopping until Christmas Eve before, and she would never do it again. If there was one thing she was good at, it was not making the same mistake twice.

Angel stepped out of the shop and planted her feet on the pavement. She shivered as the chilly winter air hit her face, feeling twice as cold as it had before she'd entered the warmth of the toy store just over an hour ago. She had gone in for one thing. Just one thing.

Why she had expected to be in and out of the store in a few minutes, she had no idea. The queues at the tills had been ridiculous, and she had come close to putting the toy back and walking out several times. Then she thought of the look on Bobby's face when he didn't get the one thing he had asked Santa to bring him for Christmas, and had known she needed to suck it up, and stick it out.

Shifting the bags she carried into one hand, she struggled to pull the zip of her jacket up underneath her chin. Angel reached behind her and grabbed the hood of the too-old winter coat she was wearing.

As she struggled to free the hood from the strap of her handbag, she found herself hoping her mum had picked up on the many not so subtle hints she'd been dropping for the last few months. She desperately needed a new winter coat, although, knowing her mum, she probably hadn't realised. She loved her mum to pieces, but even she would admit she wasn't the brightest spark around.

As she split the numerous shopping bags between her hands, she set off down the street, dodging the masses of last-minute shoppers. She was sure most of them were panic buying rather than actually putting any thought into what they were getting for their loved ones, not that anyone but them would ever know.

She may have left everything to the last minute this year, but at least she knew she had bought each person something they really wanted. Her mum was going to love the soft blue cashmere jumper, and she was pretty sure her dad was going to love her forever when he saw the new cordless drill she'd bought him.

Andy, her little brother by only two minutes, was going to go ape shit for the latest computer game she'd pre-ordered months ago. She had started to think it wouldn't be in stock in time for Christmas, but she'd gotten the call that morning, informing her it had finally arrived. Her brother had better be bloody grateful; she'd paid a small fortune for it.

Then there was Bobby. Sweet baby boy Bobby, her two-year-old little cherub. Like every mum, she'd gone way overboard with presents, but she just hadn't been able to resist all the cute clothes for little boys. She was sure he would have enough toys to enable him to play with a new one every day until next Christmas came around.

She couldn't wait to see his face when he opened all the brightly wrapped gifts. This year, he was old enough to do most of the work himself, with a little help from her, and his grandparents. Christmas morning was always a huge affair at her parents' house, and it was what Angel loved most about the whole holiday season.

Of course, she loved everything else too. The presents, the chilly winter air, the smiles that came to the faces of everyone she knew whenever a certain soft drink advert came on the TV for the first time. There was also the wide range of smells that only came with Christmas; a cooking turkey, mulled wine, and her favourite, the one given off by a real Christmas tree.

They'd always had artificial trees growing up, mainly due to the cost. Artificial trees usually lasted several years, and when they were decorated, looked just as good as a real one. However, for the last two years, since she and her brother had grown up and didn't depend on their parents as much as they used to, they'd splurged and bought a real tree. As far as she was concerned, nothing beat the fresh pine smell. Even the amount of cleaning up that was required when it shed its needles didn't put her off.

Smiling as she reached her car, Angel shifted the shopping bags back to one hand as she dug around in her handbag for her car keys. Wrapping her hand around them, she pulled them out and pressed the button, hearing the electric blue Ford KA unlock.

Releasing her grip on the keys, she opened the boot and heaved the bags up and inside, breathing a sigh of relief as the muscles in her arms silently thanked her for removing the weight they'd been carrying for the last few hours.

Angel reached into her handbag and grabbed the keys

again, but before she could open the door, she heard the familiar ringing of her phone. As she pulled it out of her pocket, she smiled when she saw who was calling, hitting the green button to answer.

"Hey, you."

"Hey, Angie. Where are you?"

Angel smiled as her best friend since nursery school used the name she knew she hated. No one called her Angie, except for Danielle, and she was sure she only did it because she knew how much it pissed her off. It had gotten to the stage that she stopped objecting to it and just accepted that Danielle was always going to call her Angie, no matter what she said to try and talk her out of it.

"I'm just loading up the car, and then I'm heading home."

"Oh no you're not, missy. I'm in town with Laura and we fancy some lunch, not to mention a cocktail or two. You up for it?"

"Lunch, I can do, but I'll have to stick to the mocktails, seeing as I'm driving."

"Can't you ring Andy to come get your car? I'm sure he owes you a favour or two."

Angel laughed at the pleading tone in Danielle's voice. She hadn't been out with the girls in a long time. They were way overdue a proper catch up, and Dani had been right when she said her brother owed her one; several, in fact. She'd bailed him out numerous times, but she knew he wouldn't be able to help her today.

Andy was having lunch with his new girlfriend. It was an 'introduce her to the parents' lunch, and part of her couldn't help but feel sorry for the girl. Her parents were hard work, unless you knew how to handle them, and she had a feeling her brother may be single again by the time lunch was over.

"You're right, he does, but he's already busy, so if you want me there, it's mocktails or nothing."

Angel heard her friend sigh and knew she would eventually give in. A sober lunch was better than no lunch at all, and she had worked up an appetite doing all that Christmas shopping.

"Fair enough. How does TGI's sound?"

Calculating how long it would take her to get there, Angel smiled when she realised she could walk it in less than ten minutes.

"Sounds good."

"Great, because we're already here, so you'd better get your ass moving. We'll have a mocktail waiting for you. Bye, babe."

Angel heard the call had ended, and she dropped the phone back into her bag. She was grateful she didn't need to move her car from the parking space she'd all but had to fight someone for that morning. She checked how long she had left on the parking ticket before walking over to the machine to extend it by three hours. That should be more than enough time to catch up with the girls.

After putting the ticket on her dashboard and locking the car, she pulled her coat closer around her neck before setting off. Less than three minutes later, she heard her phone ringing again, seeing it was Danielle. Shaking her head, Angel ignored the call and picked up the pace, figuring her friend was ringing to hurry her up.

When the phone rang again, Angel muttered under her breath and pulled the phone out, not bothering to look at the display as she answered.

"Jesus, Dani, I'm on my way. Chill out, would you?"

"Miss Mitchell?"

Angel stopped in her tracks and turned, resting against a wall as the unfamiliar voice spoke her name.

"This is Angel Mitchell. Who is this?"

"Miss Mitchell, this is Detective Sergeant Morris."

The Police? What did they want?

"Okay. How can I help you, Detective Morris?"

"There's no easy way to tell you this, Miss Mitchell, but there's been a fire at the residence of Rosemary and Trevor Mitchell. Are they your parents?"

Angel stood rooted to the spot, her vision went blurry, and her head began to spin. Her legs went numb and she slumped to the floor.

"Miss Mitchell? You need to get to Queen Elizabeth Hospital and ask for Doctor Peterson. He'll be able to update you."

"Are they…?"

Her throat closed as she tried to finish her sentence. Then it hit her.

"Bobby!" she screamed down the phone. "Please tell me my baby boy is okay."

Her breathing was rapid and her knuckles white as she clutched the phone tightly in her hand.

"You really should get to the hospital, Miss Mitchell. I regret there isn't much more I can tell you at this stage."

Angel heard the click of the call ending, but it sounded so far away. It was then she realised that she'd dropped the phone into her lap. Glancing down, she saw her hands were wet and knew it was because tears were streaming down her face.

Her parents.

Her brother.

Her baby boy.

If they were gone, nothing would ever be the same again.

CHAPTER
ONE

LESS THAN A WEEK TO GO.

Not long before he could spend the day with those he held most dear to him. They could eat lots of food, drink lots of alcohol, and generally have a great time.

He really did love this time of year. For him, it was a double celebration, seeing as almost thirty years ago he had been born on Christmas Day. He was sure that was the reason his parents had named him Gabriel. Of course, he went by Gabe. Hardly anyone used his given name, unless it was for something official. He even signed his name, *Gabe*.

School had been hellish. The bullies always came out full force at the festive time of year to make fun of his name. As soon as he'd been old enough to tell people what he wanted to be called, he'd told them he preferred Gabe, refusing to answer when anyone called him Gabriel, including his teachers. He wouldn't go as far as officially changing it, considering it disrespectful to his parents, but he did have a choice in how people addressed him.

"Hey, Gabe, we're all going for a drink after work to wet the baby's head. You in?"

Gabe turned in his chair when he heard Jake yell from right across the office, earning himself a few glares from colleagues that were on the phone. The man had a massive grin on his face, something that had been a permanent fixture ever since his wife, Charlie, had given birth to their first child, a daughter, only three days ago. All he'd done since her birth was show off pictures of little Mia, and he had to admit, she was the cutest thing he'd ever seen.

"Yeah, sure thing. Grab me on your way out."

He saw Jake give him the thumbs up and then disappear back into his office. Turning back to his computer, he decided that Christmas shopping would just have to wait for another day.

Gabe loved going out for drinks with the guys he worked with. They always had a great laugh, and even if they went out with the intention of just having one or two, it never ended up that way. At least today was a Friday, so they didn't have an early start tomorrow.

If there was one thing he hated, it was coming to work with a hangover. His boss wasn't too keen on it either. He'd been called to the carpet more than once for arriving a bit worse for wear.

Not only was it Friday, it was also his last day in work until the New Year. Every year he agreed to work over the Christmas period so that his colleagues who had kids could take the time off. This year, it was his turn to spend the holidays at home, and he couldn't deny he was looking forward to the break.

Picking up his phone to shove it in his pocket, Gabe saw he had a missed call, frowning when he saw who it was from. The number wasn't stored in his phone anymore, but it didn't need to be. No matter how hard he tried, it was one number he couldn't forget. He'd known that number for almost ten years. It wasn't miraculously going to vanish from his memory overnight, no matter how much he wished it would.

Seeing there was no voicemail and no text message, he figured she was just trying him on the off chance he'd answer. If it was anything more urgent, his phone would have been ringing non-stop and he'd have an inbox full of texts.

Just like her phone number, Gemma wasn't going to leave his memory anytime soon. There was some small part of him that was happy about that, but after everything that had happened, everything she had done, there was no way he could forgive her. She'd hurt him in one of the worst ways possible.

He was pretty sure she was the reason he was still single, and why all his relationships after her had failed. For some reason, the girls always ended things after a few months, the longest being a year, saying they needed him to be present, and they needed to know they meant something to him.

Yeah, he knew he had a problem with trust after what she had done to him, so there was no way he was going to let her back into his life.

Hitting the button to remove the little red notification from his phone screen, he put it in his pocket, and smiled. He heard them before he saw them. He knew Jake and the rest of the guys were on their way out for the weekend, and they were headed in his direction.

Shutting down his computer, he span around in his chair just as the group of five guys came to a stop by his office door.

"Let's go, Gabe," said Tom, the youngest of the bunch. "We have drinks to down and women to enjoy."

"Speak for yourself," Gabe laughed. "I'm down with the drinks, but I'll leave the women to you."

"Hey, no complaints here. More for me."

Gabe shook his head and stood, grabbing his jacket and scarf off the coat rack. With it only being a few days before Christmas, he knew the temperature outside was close to zero. He didn't plan on freezing his balls off just a few days before his favourite day of the year.

When he'd shrugged into his coat and wrapped his scarf around his neck, he turned to the group of guys who were getting a little restless.

"I'm ready when you are."

"It's about time, Gabe. Now that I have a baby to get home to, I need to take advantage of all the time I have free, and waiting around for your ass to get ready isn't how I plan on spending that time."

"Yeah, yeah. Are we going or not?"

Gabe shoved his hands in his coat pockets as he followed the others out of the office, across the foyer, and out into the cold December air. The bar they usually frequented after work was only five minutes away, but in their hurry to get out of the cold, they were inside and stripping off their coats within two.

It was no surprise to see the place was packed. Friday nights were usually busy, but add that it was getting closer to Christmas, and you had all the late-night shoppers enjoying a post-shop drink. There was standing room only.

Taking up his usual position by one of the pillars, Gabe scanned the room, looking for anyone who was close to leaving. He wasn't usually a 'swooper', but when it got this busy, needs must. He wasn't above jumping in a seat whilst the person was still getting their things together, and as if by magic, he saw two girls stand and begin to put on their coats.

With a nod, he indicated to Jake which way he was heading and weaved his way through the throng of people, coming up to the table just as the two girls slung their bags over their shoulders and turned to look up at him.

At six feet three inches, he wasn't a small guy. Both these girls couldn't have been much over five feet, so when they turned, they came face to face with his chest, before they craned their necks to look at his face. He saw the immediate interest in the deep brown eyes of the brunette, but the blonde looked completely uninterested, and that intrigued him.

He wasn't an egotist, but at the same time, he wasn't oblivious to how he looked and the affect he had on women. He had never met a woman who didn't find him attractive, yet the petite blonde standing in front of him clearly thought differently to her friend, who was practically devouring him with her eyes.

Flicking his gaze between the two women, he saw both hands were ring free. Of course, that didn't mean they weren't spoken for. Even women who were in a relationship could check out the merchandise, as long as they didn't go shopping. Talking of shopping, the brunette was laden down with bags of every description. The only bag the blonde carried was slung over her shoulder and was in no way a shopping bag.

"Ladies. A good day's shopping I see."

"You could say that," the brunette said with a smile. "Although, I was the one doing all the shopping."

"I see. So, you're a leave-it-to-the-last-minute kind of girl, then?"

Gabe directed his question to the blonde, who just gave him a look that would stop traffic, rolled her eyes, and turned to her friend.

"Can we go, Dani?"

"Um, sure."

Gabe watched as the blonde turned away and stalked through the crowd, the brunette watching her back as she went.

"Sorry about her. She's not a great fan of Christmas."

"What? How can she *not* like Christmas? I didn't think that was possible."

Gabe was unable to stop the disbelief in his tone. He'd always loved Christmas and had never met anyone who didn't feel the same. Sure, everyone liked it to different degrees, but regardless, it was always a positive feeling. It appeared this girl didn't agree, and he couldn't help but wonder why that was.

"It's not really my place to say, but this time of year holds some bad memories for her, so she just likes to lay low until it passes. Anyway, I should go catch her up. Feel free to use the table."

With those words, the brunette hurried off after her friend, thanking someone who opened the door for her. He watched as she met up with her friend outside, and the two walked off down the street.

Well, that was interesting. Two friends; one who seemed to love Christmas, the other who wasn't so keen. They must have some interesting conversations at this time of year. How could anyone not like Christmas? He just didn't get it.

Her friend had said she had some bad memories, so in a way, he could understand that. There were certain times of year he would rather miss than have to go through, but what could have happened to her to make her dislike Christmas that much?

"Way to go, Gabe. You grabbed a table."

Gabe came back to reality when he heard Jake's booming voice over the din of the crowds. He was followed by the other guys, all of whom carried a pint and a shot of a clear liquid that he figured was probably Sambuca. Jake placed his drinks down on the table and passed Gabe's over to him.

The five men circled the table and began chatting and laughing. They all toasted baby Mia, and then downed the shot of what Gabe had correctly guessed to be Sambuca. He nodded and laughed in all the right places, but his mind wasn't on the conversation his friends were having.

He couldn't erase the image of the blonde from his head.

Her distaste for the holiday season fascinated him. Gabe needed to find out more about this girl, but he had no clue what her name was or how to find her. Yet he knew he had to find out.

The only question was, how?

CHAPTER TWO

"WHAT WAS THAT ALL ABOUT?"

Angel shrugged at her friend as they walked away from the bar. She hadn't wanted to go in there in the first place, so she wasn't in any mood for some cocky guy, who clearly loved himself, trying to crack a joke about her lack of shopping bags.

Dani had dragged her into the bar after a day of Christmas shopping; shopping she hadn't known about until Dani had sprung it on her when they'd been parking. Dani had told her they were going to go for some lunch, just to get her out of the flat. By the time she'd realised what was going on, she'd had the choice to either sit in the car and wait for her friend or go shopping. She'd chosen the latter, against her better judgement, she might add, deciding anything was better than sitting in the car, on her own, for God knew how many hours.

It was a pastime she used to love, and to say she'd been pissed when Dani sprung it on her would be the understatement of the century. Dani knew how she felt about shopping, yet she'd forced it on her anyway.

Sure, she understood why people loved this time of year, and at one time, she had too. Now, every time she went out and saw the joy and happiness on people's faces as they purchased gifts for friends and family, it just reminded her of what she no longer had. Every year, Dani tried her best to help her through it, usually by attempting to keep her distracted, and whilst Angel appreciated her friend for trying, it never worked.

Christmas was never going to be the same again for her. It was just another day. She hadn't done any Christmas shopping since that day, and in all honesty, she couldn't see herself ever doing it again. What was the point when she had no one to buy for? Sure, that guy hadn't know her from Adam; had no clue about what had happened, but his comment had still struck home and only served to reinforce what she already knew.

She had no one.

"Just leave it, Dani. I'm really not in the mood."

Angel heard her friend sigh and knew there was more she wanted to say, but she was biting her tongue. Dani had been there for her when her life had come crashing down around her three years ago, but she still wasn't afraid to tell her how it was or when she was being a jerk, which was why not speaking her mind was so unlike her.

"Out with it, Dani. I know there's more you want to say."

"No. It doesn't matter."

This was also what Dani did. She'd make it clear she wanted to say something, then say nothing. It frustrated her to no end. Stopping in her tracks, Angel spun round and faced her.

"Dani, I swear to God, if you don't—"

"Fine, you really want to hear it? Then I'll tell you what everyone else around you is too scared to say. I get why you don't like Christmas, Angel, probably more than anyone, but that doesn't excuse you acting like a royal bitch to everyone who dares speak to you, or anyone who actually enjoys this time of year. That guy back there was just trying to make conversation, and you treated him like he'd just run over your favourite puppy. Seriously, Angel, I know you'll never forget what happened, but you need to find a way to move on, or you're just going to spend the rest of your life on your own because you'll have pushed away everyone who gives a damn about you, including me."

Angel watched as Dani swiped a tear from her eye and walked off into the crowds. She guessed she'd asked for that and couldn't help but wonder for how long Dani had wanted to say all of that but had held back.

Pulling her jacket closer around her, Angel took a deep breath. She needed a drink. Hell, she needed several drinks. She never drank when she drove, but tonight was definitely one of those nights where she could easily get lost in a bottle of Jack, and as she turned around, Angel saw she was only a few feet from the bar they'd just left.

"Screw it," she muttered as she moved towards the entrance and threw the door open.

She grimaced as her ears were assaulted with the sounds of cheesy Christmas music, then realised that the bar had decided to turn on its karaoke machine. The girl currently occupying the small stage, dressed in a barely there Santa dress, was trying her best to mimic Mariah Carey but failing miserably. Not that any of the guys cared. They were eating up her hip swings in the tiny, red, velvet skirt.

Finding a gap at the bar, Angel managed to grab an empty barstool and climbed on. This was going to be her spot for the rest of the night, or until she was unable to see straight and forgot why she was even there, whichever came first. Shrugging off her coat, she placed it across her lap and put her bag on the bar, just as the bartender came over.

"What can I get you?"

"A shot of Jack—and leave the bottle."

She didn't miss the look the bartender gave her as he reached over and grabbed the bottle from the shelf. Retrieving a shot glass from under the bar, he poured and put the shot in front of her. Picking it up, she downed it in one, grimacing as the liquid burned a path down her throat.

Angel slid the now empty glass over to the bartender, who just raised an eyebrow at her before pouring another, which she downed just as quickly. The amber liquid was definitely hitting the spot, and she saw the bartender smirk before doing as she asked and leaving the bottle next to her on the bar.

Truth be told, she hadn't expected him to do it, and she began to wonder whether she actually had enough money on her to cover the inevitably large bill she'd be stuck with at the end of the night.

Grabbing the bottle, Angel poured herself another shot, just as the screeching Santa on the karaoke machine finished her song. All the men hollered at her and she lapped up the attention, stepping down from the makeshift stage to be greeted by her friends as they all hugged her and jumped up and down.

At least someone is having a good time, she thought as she turned back to the full shot glass sat on the bar in front of her and quickly relieved it of its contents.

She could already feel the alcohol doing its job, and she was pretty sure that if she carried on like this, the world would be one massive blur within fifteen minutes, which was just what she was hoping for.

Angel stared into the now empty shot glass that she held in her hands, her mind drifting to the place it always went, especially at Christmastime. Images of her parents and brother filled her mind. Their happy, smiling faces the last time she saw them on the morning of the fire. Her brother's girlfriend, the only survivor, who she never got to meet. She had reached out to her several times since the fire, but to this day, Angel hadn't been able to get together the courage to speak with her, let alone go and see her.

Then there was Bobby; her angelic little boy. He had survived for several days after the fire, but his lungs had been so badly damaged that she'd had to make the decision to turn off his life support. There wasn't a day that went by when she didn't wonder if she'd made the right decision. Maybe he could have survived the injuries, despite the doctors insisting he wouldn't.

What if she'd had just a little more backbone? What if she had just stood her ground and told them no? Would Bobby have pulled through? Her baby had always been a tough little guy. If anyone could have pulled through, it was him, but she would never know now. She'd been a coward, and now her boy was gone.

Looking up from the glass, she took a deep breath, forcing back the tears threatening to fall. Grabbing hold of the bottle, she poured another shot and downed it within seconds. Angel knew if she kept going like this, she was going to have great difficulty getting home tonight. Maybe the bartender would let her sleep behind the bar, or maybe on the pool table. Didn't matter to her.

When she saw the bartender approach, she guessed it was to take the bottle of Jack from her, but instead, he placed a cocktail glass in front of her containing some kind of fruity concoction. She looked at him, the question on her face clear.

"From the guy at the end of the bar."

He smiled and left as she peered down the bar, seeing the guy she had all but dismissed earlier—at least, she thought it was the same guy smiling at her. She fought the urge to roll her eyes again and instead just forced a smile and nodded her thanks.

Angel looked at the cocktail glass in front of her, reaching out to take the stem before turning it slightly. There was a time when she drank cocktails like they were going out of fashion. She could remember many a Saturday night when she and Dani had gone out and worked their way down the cocktail menu.

Ever since she lost everything that meant anything to her, she had switched to hard liquor, hence the bottle of Jack in front of her. Cocktails just didn't hold the same appeal they once had.

"So, what happened to your friend?"

She turned at the sound of the voice and looked up at the guy from earlier. Why couldn't he just leave her alone? All she wanted to do was sit here and get blind drunk, without any interruptions. Maybe if she ignored him, he'd go away?

Angel turned back to the bottle and the cocktail in front of her, hoping the guy next to her would take the hint and just go. She could feel him standing next to her, and she had a feeling he wasn't going anywhere. Her fears were confirmed when the guy who was sat next to her stood up and walked off. She heard the stranger mutter something to him before he grabbed the stool that had just been vacated and sat down.

She knew there were only so many times she could give him the cold shoulder. She'd have to speak with him eventually, even if it was only to tell him to sling his hook and leave her alone. Deciding she was going to do just that, Angel span around on her stool, stopping suddenly when she saw him for the first time.

He might be turning out to be a right royal pain in her ass by not leaving her alone, but he was a good-looking pain in her ass. He had dark hair that was just a little too long. It fell forward over his forehead, and she watched with interest when he raised his hand and pushed it back off his face.

He wore stubble well, that much she could clearly see as his firm jawline was covered with the dark spikes, which, for some reason, had her wanting to reach out and touch them. When she lifted her eyes to his, she could see they were amused by her apparent interest; interest that she hadn't had for a man in—well, as long as she could remember. The more he smirked, the more it pissed her off, and it only made her more determined to get rid of him.

Right at this moment, though, with the alcohol swimming through her veins, she wasn't sure she had the strength or inclination to do so.

CHAPTER
THREE

GABE HAD SEEN her return almost as soon as she'd walked through the door. He had tracked her movement through the crowded room, watching when she sat down at the bar. He had furrowed his brow when she started downing shots of Jack, and cringed when the bartender left the bottle behind for her.

Whatever this girl was going through, clearly, she was hoping alcohol would help to either make it better or worse, depending on how she was viewing things. He winced again as she threw two more shots down her throat, then just stared at the bottle in front of her.

From where he was sat, he had a near perfect view of her profile. He'd seen earlier that she was a pretty girl, even if he'd only caught a brief glimpse before she'd vanished out of the doors. She had long, wavy blonde hair that she currently had pulled back from her face in a low ponytail.

He'd always had a thing for blondes, so he shouldn't really be surprised that he was so intrigued by her. Gabe just wished he could see more of that pretty face, because from what he could see, she looked sad.

Finishing his drink, he approached the bar and got the

attention of the bartender. After ordering and paying, he watched the guy deliver the cocktail to her. The expression on her face told him she hadn't been expecting it, and when she looked in his direction, he could tell the small smile and nod she gave him was just to be polite.

Okay, he needed to find out what this girl's deal was. Picking up his drink, he weaved his way through the crowds, stopping when he reached her side.

"So, what happened to your friend?"

Gabe watched her as she glanced at him briefly, before turning back to stare at the bottle of Jack still sat in front of her. He raised his eyebrows in surprise, and was about to give up and walk away, when the guy sat next to her picked up his jacket and got off the stool, indicating he could have it if he wanted.

"Cheers, mate."

Gabe sat down and angled his body, so he was facing her. He knew she would have to speak with him eventually, either to make conversation or to tell him to fuck off and leave her alone. He took a sip of his drink, just as she turned suddenly, so she was facing him.

He expected her to lay into him, but instead, she just looked at him, and it was a look he'd seen before. Despite her eyes looking glassy from the alcohol she'd consumed, he saw the dilation in her pupils as her eyes searched his face. He was unable to stop the smirk from appearing on his lips, and the amusement in his eyes must have shown, because as soon as her gaze lifted to his, her expression changed from interested to pissed off in one second flat.

Now he really thought she would tell him where to go, but instead she just poured herself another shot, downed it, poured another, and slid it across to him.

"If you're going to sit there and expect me to talk, you need to catch up."

Gabe looked at the shot glass in front of him, and the

amber liquid it contained. He wasn't really a fan of Jack, of any kind of whiskey really, but if it meant she would talk to him and not send him packing, he would suck it up, despite the consequences of the inevitable hangover he'd have tomorrow.

Picking up the small glass, Gabe downed the shot, trying but failing to hide his grimace as the liquid burned a path down his throat. When his eyes stopped watering, he looked at the girl, seeing she was now smiling, amusement sparking in her eyes.

"I'm glad to see my discomfort amuses you," Gabe said as he took a large gulp of his beer to try and get rid of the taste in his mouth.

When he was sure he wasn't going to gag, Gabe looked at her again, seeing for the first time how beautiful she really was. She had high cheekbones that had a rosy glow to them, a glow that was either natural or drink induced. Her full lips were tipped upwards in a small smile, and even though her blue eyes now sparkled, he could see they were still haunted by something.

Her friend had indicated that this was a bad time of year for her, and if that were true, he had a feeling the trying to drink herself into oblivion was tied into it somehow.

"You're not a Jack drinker, are you? I think you're the first guy I've met who doesn't like the stuff."

"Whiskey and I are not friends—well, ever since my eighteenth birthday, that is. Before then, we were inseparable."

Gabe flashed her a smile, just to see if he would get one in return, and was pleasantly surprised when he did. Despite the fact she appeared to be relaxing a little, and he knew it was none of his business, he was still curious as to why she was in here alone, determined to drink herself stupid.

"You seem to be on good terms with Jack. Any reason for that? Pretty girl like you drinking alone at this time of year can't be good."

He saw the smile fade from her face as soon as the statement passed his lips. She said nothing for several moments, instead choosing to pour them both another shot, before downing hers quickly.

"Yeah well, Jack helped me get through some shit times, so saying we're on good terms is probably a huge understatement." She downed his shot when he didn't drink it, before continuing, "You could say Jack is the only real friend I have right now, especially at this time of year."

Gabe hadn't failed to notice the slur to her voice as she spoke. She'd said what she had so matter of factly, he had the impression she was trying not to think about why Christmas was such a tough time for her.

"Your friend who was here earlier seemed to care about you. She looked worried, or did I get that wrong?"

"Ah Dani. You know, Dani and I have known each other forever. She's the one person I can trust to call me out when I'm being a bitch, which, by the way, is what she did earlier. It's also why I'm in here drinking myself stupid at a time of year that I despise more than you could ever know."

Gabe nodded at her words, maintaining eye contact with her until she returned to staring at the bottle that now only contained enough of the amber liquid for another couple of shots.

He couldn't deny that his curiosity about what had caused her to be so melancholy was getting the better of him. He didn't know her well enough to just come out and ask her, and he had a feeling she wouldn't tell him even if he did, which meant one thing.

He needed to get her to trust him. He needed to get her to open up, and then convince her why she should love Christmas, despite what she had been through.

And he only had a few days in which to do it.

CHAPTER FOUR

WHAT THE HELL had she drunk last night? Scratch that, how *much* had she drunk last night?

Her head felt like someone was playing a huge ass drum kit in her skull, and her mouth was like the Sahara. Angel opened her eyes, grimacing as the light from outside hit them, and she flung her arm up to cover them.

Jesus, she felt rough. She hadn't felt this bad in a long time. She knew it was going to be a while before she felt human again, and she thanked God she had nowhere to be today. At least, she didn't think she did. Her memory was foggy, to say the least. Alcohol had a tendency to poke holes in her memory. She only wished it would do that to the things in her past she really wanted to forget.

"Wakey, wakey, sleepy head."

Angel heard the voice, which sounded vaguely familiar, and sat upright in bed. The haze that the bright light created in front of her eyes began to clear, and she stared up at the man from the bar. At least, that's where she thought she knew him from. The question was, what the hell was he doing in her bedroom, wearing just his jeans, carrying two cups of what she hoped contained coffee.

"What the hell are you doing here?"

She tracked him as he crossed the room, trying her hardest to keep her eyes on his face and not on the perfectly formed pecs and toned stomach that were covered in lightly tanned skin. When he sat on the chair by the side of her bed, he placed a cup of what she now knew was definitely coffee on her bedside table.

He leaned back in the seat and lifted his legs, propping his bare feet on the edge of her bed, crossing them at the ankles as he sipped his own coffee.

"What am I doing here? Well, you were pretty wasted last night. You could hardly stand, and you didn't know where you were. What kind of gentleman would I have been if I had left you to get home alone?"

Angel narrowed her eyes at him, moving her hands to put them on her hips, a posture that would have been more effective if she were standing and not still in bed. When her hands connected with denim, she saw she was still fully dressed. The only thing missing were her shoes. She could see them neatly placed in front of her wardrobe, and damn it, she hated it when she realised she was actually disappointed that nothing appeared to have happened between them the night before, despite his shirtless state.

She took a deep breath, preparing to tell him to get out, but her nostrils were filled with the delicious aroma of bacon.

"Are you cooking?"

The guy, whose name she still didn't know, or at least couldn't remember, removed his feet from her bed and sat forward. She really wished he would stop moving. It was only making his muscles flex, distracting her from being pissed at him. Unless that was his intention.

"I figured if you're anything like everyone else I know, when you get a hangover—which I can see you have from the way you're squinting your eyes at the light—you'll want a nice, greasy fry-up to combat it. Am I wrong?"

Damn it, he was right. She loved a fry-up when she was hungover. The only thing she didn't like about one was the fact she needed to cook it. She usually went to the café around the corner. Angel had been there so often recently that she didn't even need to order. The owner knew what she wanted off by heart. More often than not, she was still too drunk to care about how predictable she was becoming, especially when a plate full of food was placed on the table almost as soon as she sat down.

"Three sausages, two rashers of bacon, two eggs, beans, tomatoes, black pudding, and heavy on the mushrooms. Now get out of my bedroom so I can shower and change."

He just looked at her for a moment—before he burst out laughing. The noise was deep and rich, and hell if it didn't make a swarm of butterflies take flight in her stomach. She hadn't felt a reaction like this to a guy in a very long time, and she hoped he would get out of there soon, otherwise she'd be tempted to invite him into the shower with her.

He took several moments to drink the rest of his coffee before giving her a salute, standing, and crossing the room, heading towards the door.

"Hey," she called out, causing him to stop and turn around. "What's your name?"

The guy just smiled as he walked—no, he sauntered into her kitchen. All she could do was watch the muscles work across his back, knowing she was still none the wiser as to who this guy was, or why he had taken an interest in her.

Twenty minutes later, Angel was fresh from the shower, dressed in her favourite loungewear, and starting to feel almost human. She walked through to the kitchen, spying folded up blankets on the sofa, indicating he had slept out here last night.

She inwardly winced, knowing that couldn't have been comfortable for him. He was well over six feet tall, and her sofa wasn't built for someone of his size to sleep on. Still, as she watched him putting two plates on her kitchen table, where two glasses of orange juice already sat, and her untouched cup of coffee, he didn't seem any worse for wear.

He had put on his shirt from last night—at least, she assumed it was the one he wore last night—but had it unbuttoned. He was more covered up now than he had been earlier, but somehow, he looked sexier with the shirt on than he did without it.

"Feel better?" he asked, when he saw her approach the table.

"Yes, thanks. Looks good—the food, I mean."

Why she had felt the need to clarify her statement, she didn't know, because she did think he looked good. Angel had never been one to shy away from saying what she felt when it came to men. She had always been the one to make the first move if she was interested—not that she'd been interested in a while—and it usually got her what she wanted, but with him it felt different, and she couldn't put her finger on why.

Ignoring the smirk that was now on his face, Angel pulled out a chair and sat in front of one of the plates, reaching out to grab the glass so she could take a sip of the juice. She watched as he sat opposite her, picking up his knife and fork before he started eating.

He had already eaten one of the sausages and was working his way through his second piece of toast before she had chance to pick up her utensils. Clearly, he also liked a fry-up after a night of drinking. Then again, she only actually remembered him having one drink. He'd only drunk one of the shots she had pushed in front of him, and she didn't recall him ordering any more after he had finished the beer he'd had when he approached her.

Angel began eating the breakfast he had prepared for her, surprised when the silence didn't bother her as much as it usually did. It was almost comfortable sitting here eating with him, even though he was as good as a stranger. Granted, he was a very-easy-on-the-eyes stranger, but a stranger nonetheless.

After a short while, they both finished eating, and Angel believed that her hangover had almost gone. All she needed to do now was finish her coffee, and the transformation from hungover zombie to almost normal human being would be complete.

When he reached over and picked up her plate, Angel sat forward and grabbed his wrist to stop him.

"No, you cooked. The least I can do is clean up."

He looked at her for a moment, before putting her plate back on the table and resuming his sitting position, holding his hands up as if surrendering. Angel picked up her own plate before grabbing his and making her way over to the sink. She frowned when she realised he had already washed up the frying pan, and the other pans he had used. They were piled neatly on the draining board, so all she had to do was wash the plates and cutlery.

Angel knew that task would only take her a few minutes, so she placed the items in the bowl and began to run the water, waiting for it to fill. She looked up and out of the window, seeing his reflection in the glass. He was still sat at the table, but he had turned his body so that he was watching her.

His legs were stretched out in front of him, with his feet crossed at the ankles, just like they had been earlier in her bedroom. One of his arms rested on the table, the other on the arm of the chair. She had no idea whether he could see her watching him, and frankly, she didn't care if he did.

As she studied him, she couldn't figure out why he was still here. Why was he hanging around, and even worse, why hadn't she kicked him out yet? After she'd all but dismissed him at the bar yesterday, he'd sought her out when she'd returned, sat with her while she'd drunk herself stupid, and escorted her home safely. If what he had told her earlier was to be believed.

Angel knew she should be saying thank you and goodbye right about now, but there was something inside stopping her, and that both intrigued her and pissed her off in equal measure.

CHAPTER
FIVE

HE KNEW she was watching him. He also knew that, going by the way she had reacted to him yesterday, he was lucky to still be there with his balls intact. He had expected her to throw him out as soon as she realised he was there, so the fact he was still here, sat in her kitchen, after just enjoying breakfast with her, baffled him.

To say she had been worse for wear last night would be a major understatement. She had polished off the bottle of Jack she'd had in front of her and had asked the bartender for another, but he had cut her off, which had caused many protests from her before she'd finally relented. When she had tried to stand up to leave, her legs gave out, and he'd had to catch her.

He had settled her bill, leaving him almost £100 down, then helped her outside, where she had promptly thrown up most of the alcohol she had consumed into the gutter, before he had guided her into a taxi. He had found her address and her name from her driving license, and the journey had, thankfully, been relatively short. Her head was on his shoulder as she had mumbled incoherently about someone called Bobby.

When he had managed to get her inside, thanking God that she lived on the ground floor, he had wandered around to find her bedroom, sat her down, removed her shoes, and she had passed out almost instantly. He'd had a pretty crappy night's sleep, as he had decided he couldn't leave her in that state, so he had tried to get comfy on her sofa. A sofa he had quickly found out wasn't designed for someone of his size.

Gabe had checked on her several times during the night, seeing that she had somehow managed to get under the covers but was still sleeping soundly. He'd been unable to settle, so had wandered around her flat, surprised to see it quite sparsely furnished. There were no photos or the usual knick-knacks that girls usually had dotted around. A few boxes were stacked in the corner, still sealed up with parcel tape.

Maybe she had just moved in? That could explain it. It only made him more curious. Where had she come from? What prompted her move, and who was this guy, Bobby, that she had been mumbling about the night before?

When she stopped watching him and started washing the breakfast items, he sat up straight and leaned forward, deciding that if he ever wanted to learn anything about this girl—and he knew he did—he needed to grow a pair and start asking some questions.

"Who's Bobby?"

Her reaction was instantaneous. She dropped the plate she'd been holding, and he watched as it fell through the air, shattering as it hit the kitchen floor. She whirled around, her eyes landing on him as she moved forward. She stopped in front of him, and he sat back in the chair. Gabe could almost feel the emotion coming off her in waves. Her hands were balled into fists at her sides, and there was a fire in her eyes that, if he had to guess, was a mixture of anger and pain.

"Don't you dare speak his name! You have no right to talk about him. Get out!"

She screamed the words right into his face, and he was torn between honouring her request to leave or staying to try and calm her down. He figured the latter was going to be worse for his health, as she looked ready to kill him, but it was the one he was leaning towards. This girl was clearly hurting, and whoever Bobby was, he had to be the cause of that hurt.

"Whoa. Calm down."

"Didn't you hear me? Get. The fuck. Out!"

The look on her face was murderous, and when she started pummelling his chest with her fists, he could see the tears streaming down her face. Being tall came with advantages, one of which being strength. As she continued to pound at his chest, Gabe just stood and wrapped his arms around her, effectively stopping her actions and pinning her arms between them.

"Let me go!" she shouted as she struggled against him.

"Sssh. It's okay. Whatever it is, let it out."

"No! Just let me go!"

She continued to fight him for several more minutes, determined to get away from him, but eventually, he felt her give in as her body sagged against him, and the tears came thick and fast. He loosened his hold on her slightly when he felt her trying to move her arms and was surprised when she wrapped them around his waist and cried into his chest.

oOo

"I lost everything that day. Everyone I ever loved, gone, just like that."

Gabe sat opposite her on the sofa and listened as she spoke. When she had calmed down, Gabe released his hold on her, and she'd moved to the living room as he made two fresh mugs of coffee. When he'd joined her, she recounted what had happened three years ago, fighting the tears throughout.

If he had to guess, he would say this was the first time she had spoken with anyone about what happened, and he now understood why she felt the way she did about this time of year. And he couldn't blame her. He remembered reading about the fire in the news, recalling how a faulty electrical cable had caused the inferno. It had spread so quickly that no one inside had stood a chance.

Angel had told him her brother's girlfriend had survived, despite having severe burns and smoke inhalation. She had spent several weeks in the hospital before being discharged to the care of her parents. As far as Angel knew, she had moved on with her life, something Angel herself was struggling to do.

"I can't begin to understand what you've gone through," Gabe said to her as she hugged her knees to her chest, balancing her mug on the arm of the sofa. "I know that couldn't have been easy for you to tell me, considering you don't really know me."

"Yeah, well. I figured I owed you an explanation for going off on you earlier, when all you did was ask who Bobby was. He was my life. I didn't have much, but I had him, and he made everything I did worthwhile." She took a deep breath before continuing. "Even now, after all this time, whenever I close my eyes, I can see his happy, smiling face, and it's like he's right here with me. When I open them, I remember what happened, and the pain hits me all over again."

She was crying again now, the tears slipping silently down her cheeks. He didn't think, he just reached out and took her free hand in his, giving it a gentle squeeze as they just sat there.

They sat there for at least thirty minutes, each sipping their coffee with their free hand whilst their other hands were clasped together on the cushions between them. It was Gabe who broke the silence.

"I lost a child too."

CHAPTER
SIX

ANGEL TURNED to him when she heard his words, seeing him looking straight ahead. He still held her hand in his, and his thumb was moving over her knuckles in slow, even strokes. It was almost as if holding her hand was keeping him grounded, and all she could do was listen as he shared his story with her, like she had just done with him.

"Gemma and I had been together since high school. We were both fourteen when we met. At first, it was just a crush, but the older we got, those feelings developed into love, and by eighteen, we were engaged. We'd spoken about having a family loads of times but agreed we would wait until we were a bit older, as we both wanted to finish college and have at least one of us with a decent job before we brought kids into the picture. Anyway, about eighteen months later, Gemma told me she was pregnant. I was shocked, but at the same time, I was so happy, and I thought she was too."

. . .

Angel felt the grip he had on her hand tighten as he shifted restlessly, turning his head to look at her as he continued.

"The weeks passed, and I started buying bits and pieces for the baby. My family did too. Just small things like bibs and rattles. By the time Gemma was sixteen weeks, she still wasn't showing, so I suggested we go to the doctors for a scan, just to see if everything was okay. She told me it wasn't unusual for there to be no baby bump at that stage, and thought up every excuse under the sun as to why it wasn't necessary to go and have a scan, but this was our first child, and I wanted to make sure everything was okay, so I was pretty insistent."

She knew what was coming next, and if she had to guess, it was something he hadn't spoken about in a long time.

"I was relentless. I kept telling her it was my baby too, and I wanted some reassurance that everything was okay. I pushed, and I pushed, until she snapped and shouted that she wasn't pregnant. Not anymore. I didn't understand what she was telling me at first. I just stood there and looked at her. I asked her what she meant, and that was when she told me she'd had an abortion a little over three weeks before."

Now it was her turn to squeeze his hand. What he had gone through, while completely different to her situation, clearly hurt him as much as losing Bobby had hurt her. Neither of them had been given a choice in the loss of their children. His hadn't even entered this world, yet it was clear from the way he was trying to hold back the tears that he still loved that child.

. . .

"I guess we've both been screwed over by the powers that be, huh?"

"Yeah, you could say that. I've never told anyone outside of my family that story."

"Same here, apart from Dani, I mean."

"I understand now why you're not a huge fan of this time of year. It must bring back painful memories."

All she could do was nod as she swallowed the lump that was forming in her throat—not for the first time that morning.

"I get it, I do, but you can't live your life in the past, Angel. You need to find a way to remember Bobby, but also be able to enjoy your life, especially Christmas."

Angel heard the words, and before he had even finished, she was already shaking her head. "No, too much has happened. I can't just get on with things as if everything is normal, when it isn't."

"No one is asking you to forget what's happened, but—"

She pulled her hand from his and stood, turning to face him. She could feel herself shaking, and she knew she was only moments from completely breaking down. She needed him gone, and she needed it to be now.

"I said no, so stop trying to force this on me. If I want to stay indoors and drown myself in drink until the season is through, then I will. If I want to sit and look at pictures of my baby boy and my family, and work my way through several boxes of tissues, I will. It's got nothing to do with you, so don't for one minute think that just because I told you about my tragic past, you can tell me what to do, and how I should get over it. Now, I'd appreciate it if you'd leave. I have things I need to do."

Angel watched as he stared at her for a few moments, not moving and not saying anything. She was half expecting him to refuse again, but he eventually stood and started gathering his things. After less than five minutes, he was slipping his arms into his coat and walking to the door. He opened it, but stopped, and turned to face her.

"You're right, Angel, I do love Christmas, and I'm willing to bet that before you lost your family, you did too. I will leave you alone for now, as it's been an emotional morning, for both of us, but let me make one thing clear right now. I will be back, and I will make you see why you used to love Christmas." He paused again, before saying one last thing. "Bobby might have only been a toddler when you lost him, but I know he wouldn't want his mum to be unhappy, Angel. I think you know that too."

With those words, he stepped out of the room, and the door closed. After a few moments, Angel took a deep breath, and released it with a loud scream, resisting the urge to throw her half-full coffee mug across the room.

· · ·

Who did this guy think he was? What right did he have to come into her home and tell her how to grieve for her family? She still had no idea who this guy was, or why he was so intent on inserting himself into her life.

In the short time she'd known him, he had spent more time pissing her off than anything else, but one thing she was slowly beginning to realise was that he wasn't just going to go away because she told him to. She would be seeing more of him; of that she was sure. All she had to do was prove to him that she had every right to feel the way she did, and if he didn't like it, he could just go back to wherever he came from.

CHAPTER
SEVEN

GABE KNEW he'd been pushing his luck, and that it was only a matter of time before she had enough and asked him to go. Even now, almost twelve hours after leaving her, he still couldn't stop thinking about her and what she'd been through.

It was not surprising that she felt down and a little withdrawn at this time of year. She'd lost her parents, her brother, and her son. Anyone who had been through what she'd been through would feel the same, but he was still struggling to get his head around why she seemed to blame the whole Christmas season and refused to at least try and enjoy herself.

Sighing deeply, Gabe punched his pillow a few times and threw the covers off his body. Considering the temperature outside had dropped to below freezing, it was like an oven in his bedroom, and he started to wonder whether he was coming down with something.

Having a cold or the flu over Christmas wasn't something he enjoyed. It had happened once before, and it had put a real downer on the whole day. He hadn't been able to enjoy his Christmas dinner because he'd not been able to taste it. All the usual wintery smells—the pine from the tree, turkey cooking in the oven—had been absent, and to top it all, he'd agreed to pick up his sister and her children, so he couldn't even have a drink to drown his sorrows. No, being ill at Christmas wasn't at the top of his to do list.

As he stared into the darkness, the room got a little brighter when his phone lit up to indicate a message. He reached over to pick it up, seeing it was a message from the same number he was trying his hardest to forget. Against his better judgement, Gabe slid his thumb across the screen to unlock it, and opened the messaging app.

Why she had suddenly started contacting him now, and at one in the morning, he had no idea. Before her phone call on Friday, he'd heard nothing from Gemma for several months. Now she was calling and texting him again, which usually meant she wanted something, or she had been dumped by whichever guy she had been seeing.

He never responded to her messages, or returned her calls, but right now, he couldn't help but wonder why she was getting in touch after so long. Radio silence with Gemma only normally lasted a few weeks, a couple of months at the most. His parents had always told him his curious nature would come back and bite him sooner or later, and he knew that this could be one of those times.

Opening her brief yet to the point message of, *Hey, how are you?* Gabe typed a response of, *I'm okay. How are you?* knowing that this would be the first time in many years he would have interacted with the woman who all but destroyed his life. He also knew he could quite possibly be opening the floodgates to a whole flurry of calls and messages from her in the coming days and weeks.

She responded after a few minutes with an emoji showing she was surprised he had responded, along with a message that was instantly making him regret answering her. It was also making him worry about a certain blonde that had recently come into his life.

Wow! I can't believe you actually responded to my message. I figured you would just ignore me again, like you always do. You always did think you were better than me. So, what's changed, huh? What made you decide to reply to me this time? Are you up in your bedroom, all alone? Probably having a wank. I mean, let's face it, it's all you did when we were together. If it wasn't Sports Illustrated, it was one of those filthy porn websites. Maybe that pretty little blonde you met last night can help you? Mind you, she did look like she had more interest in drinking than she did in you. What went wrong, losing your touch? The only way you could get her to take you back to her place was because she was too pissed to stop you. Still as pathetic as ever, I see. Sometimes I wonder what I ever saw in you. Oh well, at least she saw sense and kicked you to the kerb, but not until you got to stay the night. What happened? Did she wake up, realise what she'd done, and throw you out, or did you piss her off with your 'me, me, me' whining? At least you made it until lunchtime, not bad going I suppose. Anyway, I just wanted to check in, make sure you were still alive. Toodles.

What the fuck! How the hell did she know about Angel, and how did she know about what had happened last night, and this morning? Sure, she could have guessed, but that was a lot of information to just think up out of nowhere and have it all be correct. As he read her message again, he wondered what had gone so wrong in her life for her to be so nasty in her response to him.

The Gemma he had known had been a sweet girl. She would do anything for anyone, and she wouldn't say boo to a goose. This Gemma, the one that had sent him that message, wasn't the same girl he had known. He knew a lot could happen over the years, and people could change, but this change was so drastic, he knew something big must have caused it.

And then there was Angel. The only way Gemma could know the things she did was if she had been there last night. Could she have followed them from the bar to Angel's place?

Had she stayed out there all night to see him leave the next morning, or had that just been a guess? Either way, he was worried about Angel, a girl he hardly knew.

He was tempted to go around there and make sure she was okay. Or at least make sure no one was lurking around outside her flat. It was late, so anyone wandering around would be easily noticeable. Maybe he could just drive past and check? At least that would put his mind at rest.

Jumping out of bed, Gabe pulled on his jeans, threw on an old t-shirt, and moved through to the kitchen to grab his keys off the counter. Within a few minutes, he was in his car and driving the short distance to Angel's flat.

He knew he was probably overreacting. Gemma was just trying to get a reaction out of him. Gabe knew she still lived in the area, so it was possible she had seen him at the bar with Angel and just assumed something had gone on with them, but that didn't explain how she had known what time he had left her place.

Pushing the accelerator, Gabe turned the corner and saw Angel's place in the distance. He slowed the car, making sure he scanned the street as he went by. He didn't see anyone walking about. In fact, the place was eerily quiet. Even at this hour, he still expected to see a few people, but there was no one, which, in a way, was a good thing.

As he neared her building, Gabe pulled up across the street and switched off the engine. He could see there was a light on in Angel's flat, even though the curtains were drawn. He was tempted to go over and knock, but he had a feeling she wouldn't appreciate him showing up at this hour, especially after their earlier disagreement.

Even if he did go up there, what would he say? *Hey, just wanted to check you were okay, and that my ex-girlfriend—you know, the one I mentioned earlier, and who seems to be a bit crazy—wasn't lurking in the darkness watching you.* Yeah, that would go down well. He had a feeling he was already on her 'steer clear' list, so he didn't want to do anything that might push her even further away from him.

Deciding he was being paranoid, Gabe turned on the engine and pulled away, all the while thinking of ways he could get back in Angel's good books. He meant what he had said when he'd been leaving her place; he would make her love Christmas again. He just had to figure out how.

CHAPTER
EIGHT

"DANI, I really don't want to."

"Oh, come on, Angel. You can't leave me on my own with four kids. I promise not to ask anything of you again until after Christmas. Just this one thing. Please?"

Angel fell back onto her sofa and closed her eyes. She knew this phone call had been coming. Dani did it every year. She agreed to take her four nieces for the day so that her sisters could get their Christmas shopping done, and then somehow talked her into helping her with said nieces.

She always protested, Dani always begged, and the outcome was always the same: she gave in to her friend, no matter how much she really didn't want to go. Part of her wondered why they did this song and dance every year. She should just say yes as soon as Dani called her, it would save all this going backward and forward.

· · ·

"Fine. What time, and where?"

"Yay! Thank you, Angel. You know you have a good time when you get here. I'll meet you at the ice rink in an hour. Is that okay?"

Angel glanced down at her pyjama clad body and mentally calculated how long it would take her to get ready, and then get to the ice rink.

"Make it an hour and a half."

"Still in your PJs, huh?"

"Shut up. I'll see you later."

When Dani started to laugh, Angel ended the call, but couldn't stop a small smile from appearing on her face. She could always rely on Dani to call her out. Sometimes Angel hated that her friend knew her so well. Of course, it probably had something to do with all the weekends they'd spent together, when they'd lounged around in their pyjamas practically all day.

Tossing her phone onto the sofa next to her, Angel got to her feet and went through to the bathroom. After a quick shower, she walked into her bedroom and climbed onto the bed. She really didn't want to go out today, but now that she had told Dani she would, she couldn't back out of it.

If it was just her and Dani, there wouldn't be a problem, but with Dani's four nieces in tow, she knew she would be coming home later with one hell of a headache. The girls were aged between five and eleven, and when they got on, they were angels, but more often than not, they argued, and spending time with four squealing girls wasn't high on her to do list.

Still, she had committed to going, so come hell or high water, she would be at that ice rink in… she checked her watch; just under an hour. Resisting the urge to fall back on the bed and get comfy amongst the pillows, Angel dragged herself back to her feet and pulled on some socks. Once she'd slipped into her underwear, she grabbed a pair of jeans, a plain white t-shirt, and her favourite soft lilac cardigan out of her chest of drawers. She was dressed within five minutes and unwrapped the towel from around her hair as she grabbed her hairdryer.

As she looked at herself in the mirror, she switched on the dryer and let the hot air breeze through her long hair. She'd decided to wear it up, so it was out of her face, so she wasn't too fussed about it being perfectly dry.

When it was done, Angel threw the mass of hair up into a high ponytail and applied a touch of mascara to her lashes. She didn't want to go out, but seeing as she had no choice, she at least wanted to look halfway decent. She applied a light pink lip gloss and knowing the brisk wind gusting outside would give her cheeks a rosy glow, she didn't apply the blush.

She nodded at her reflection when she was done, before standing and walking over to her wardrobe to retrieve her boots. Angel loved wearing these boots at this time of year. The well-worn black leather was so comfy, and the fleece lining gave her legs some warmth when the temperature dropped.

Angel knew the drive to the ice rink was about twenty minutes, so she needed to leave now if she had any hope of being able to park when she got there. Slipping her arms into her coat, she buttoned it up to her neck, forgoing a scarf, then slung her bag over her shoulder after fishing out her keys.

Grabbing her phone from where she'd left it on the sofa, Angel opened her front door, jumping when she nearly walked straight into the person who was just about to knock.

"What are you doing here?"

Angel looked up into the same eyes she'd peered into yesterday. He lowered his arm and took a step back, shoving his hands into the back pockets of his jeans. When he didn't answer straightaway, Angel took a moment to take in his appearance; black jeans, black button-down shirt, black jacket. When you added in his dark hair, deep brown eyes, and the stubble that still lined his jaw, he made a very appealing package, no matter how much she wished he didn't.

"Um, I came to apologise for yesterday. You heading out?"
    "Wow. You could be Sherlock Holmes. How did you guess that?"

. . .

Angel rolled her eyes and stepped forward so she could close her front door. When she was sure it was locked, she started off down the short corridor that led to the main doors, well aware that the man in black was following close behind her.

"Yeah, stupid question I know. Where are you going?"
"What's it to you?"
"Just curious. You look really nice, by the way."

Angel tried to think of a witty comeback, but she was so surprised by his compliment that it threw her off balance. She stopped walking as she neared the door and turned to him. She wasn't sure how to respond. Should she just thank him or tell him he looked nice too? If she didn't acknowledge it, would she seem petty? Then again, she'd already seen his ego at play in the bar; she didn't need to massage it any further.

"Thanks." She paused for a moment, then decided it couldn't do any harm to tell him where she was going. "I'm going ice skating with a friend."
"That sounds fun. Can I come?"

Angel shot him a look of disbelief, before answering, "Um, let me think. No."
"Oh, come on. I've nothing else planned for today, and I've not been ice skating for years."
"Really? You came all the way over here dressed like that, and you've nothing else planned for today. Why don't I believe you?"

"Dressed like what?"

Angel rolled her eyes again and huffed out a breath in frustration. Trust him to pick that small part out of the sentence. She couldn't really say, *'like you stepped off the cover of a magazine,'* to him. That would really send his ego soaring.

"Well, you're a little overdressed just to come around and say sorry. If I didn't know any better, I'd say you came around for something else."

Not giving him a chance to reply, Angel put her hand on the door and pushed it open. She stepped out into the cold winter air and knew he was still behind her. He was being unusually quiet right now. Back in the bar, from what she could remember, and the morning after, he'd been quite talkative, now it was like he was a different guy.

"Okay, you got me. I did come around to apologise—an apology you've still not accepted, by the way—but I also wanted to ask you to lunch."

"Fine, apology accepted, but as you can see, I'm heading out, so I'm afraid lunch is out of the question."

"It would be, unless you let me come with you. Come on, it will be fun."

Jesus, this guy was relentless. Angel checked her watch, knowing she couldn't stay here and argue with him much longer. She had to leave now, otherwise she was going to struggle to park at the ice rink. She had to give him an answer. Angel had a feeling that if she just ignored him and drove off, he would probably jump in his car and follow her.

She wanted to stick to her guns and tell him to back off and leave her be, but as she looked at him, she found she was unable to do that. There was an almost pleading look on his handsome face, and yes, she could admit he was handsome, so against her better judgement, she made a decision.

"Fine, get in. I'm driving."

Angel saw the beaming smile spread across his face as she unlocked her car. She walked around to the driver's side and watched as he folded his large frame into her little Ford KA. When she climbed in herself, she nearly burst out laughing at the sight that greeted her.

Even with the seat pushed right back, there was very little room for him to stretch his legs, so his knees looked like they came up to his chest. His head was only an inch or so from the roof, and the look he was giving her was one that said, *'Seriously!'*

"Oh, come on, Angel, you can't expect me to travel to the ice rink like this. Let's take my car. It has more than enough room to swing a cat."

"Hey, don't go trash talking Ethel. This car has been a good little runner for me. It's not her fault you're freakishly tall."

"Ethel? You call your car Ethel?"

"Yup, after my nan."

"I have a feeling there's a story there."

"There is, but you're not going to hear it. Now get comfy, we need to get going."

"Comfy? That's not going to happen, sweetheart. Please, Angel, can we go in my car?"

It took a few moments for Angel to respond to his question. Her brain was still processing that he had called her 'sweetheart'. She knew it meant nothing, and it was just something men called women, even one's they hardly knew, but it still sounded, dare she say it, good coming from his lips.

"Fine. Anything to stop you whinging all the way there."

"Thank God."

He was out of the car within seconds and sprinting across the street. Before she even had chance to lock her car, he had brought his over and was now waiting a few feet away for her to join him. She had heard someone say once that you could tell a lot about a man by the car he drove, and that the car reflected the man's personality.

She looked at the sleek black Mercedes that was polished to within an inch of its short life, if the registration plate was anything to go by. As she neared, she saw him reach across, and the passenger door opened. She hesitated slightly before sliding into the cream leather seat, the warmth from the heater doing wonders to warm her chilly body.

. . .

"All set?"

Angel nodded as he revved the engine and the car roared to life. While she didn't know much about the man sat next to her, she did know this: the car definitely reflected the man. Dark, powerful, and sexy. She had a feeling she was in for one hell of a ride.

CHAPTER
NINE

AS HE DROVE to the ice rink, Gabe was still a little amazed at how easy it had been to convince her to let him come along. He hadn't been lying when he said he'd gone around there to ask her to lunch. It was the reason he had made such an effort in his appearance this morning.

It had taken him more than half an hour to decide what to wear, which had surprised him as he usually grabbed whatever he laid his hands on first. When he had seen her reaction to his appearance—a reaction he didn't think she had been aware of—he knew taking the extra time had been worth it.

He still wasn't sure what it was about this girl that made him want to make the effort, but despite her initial hesitations, the fact that she had relented and let him come along today was a huge step in the right direction. Although, what direction that was, he still wasn't sure.

. . .

Gabe knew he wanted to get to know this girl better, but he still hadn't decided if it would go any further than friendship. Sure, he was attracted to her—he didn't know a guy who wouldn't be—but she didn't seem to be in a place where she was looking for anything more, even if he did want to take it further.

As he indicated left and turned off the main road, he glanced across at her, seeing her playing a game on her phone.

"What level are you on?"
 "Um, 3476."
 "Wow, seriously? I think I'm stuck somewhere in the five hundreds."
 "You've got some catching up to do then, haven't you? We're here."

Gabe looked up, seeing the entrance to the ice rink in front of him. He pulled in and surprisingly found a parking space pretty easily. As he was turning off the engine, he heard Angel speaking on her phone.

"Hey, Dani. Yeah, I'm here. Where are you? Okay, see you in five."
 "Dani is the girl from the bar, right?"
 "Yeah, that's her. She's waiting by the skate rental stand."

She quickly jumped out of the car as if it were on fire and strode off in the direction of the ice rink. He caught up with her after a few seconds, his long legs easily keeping up with her brisk pace. Was she in a hurry to get to her friend or just trying to lose him in the crowds? Either way, she wasn't going to escape from him that easily.

After a few moments, he saw Angel wave at someone and spotted the woman he had met at the bar, seeing her eyebrows rise into her hairline when she noticed him walking alongside her friend. He also saw four young girls surrounding the friend, and he looked down at Angel as they neared.

"Um, you didn't mention anything about kids coming too."

Angel looked up at him and gave him a small smile. "Didn't I? Oops."

Gabe continued looking at her before smiling. Oh, she got him good and proper, and judging by the smile that was still on her face, she was enjoying this. He glanced in her direction again, noticing there was something different about this smile compared to all the others she had given him since they met. This smile was genuine.

"Angel! I'm so happy you could come. You remember the girls?"

"I do," Angel said as she hugged her friend, who still had her eyes on him. "How are you, girls? Excited to go skating?"

· · ·

There was a chorus of *'yes'* from the girls as they all jumped up and down excitedly. Angel stepped back, and when she made no move to introduce him, Gabe stepped forward.

"Hi, we met briefly the other night. I'm Gabe."

"Dani. It's nice to see you again, although I'm a little surprised to see you with Angie here."

"Me too," he said as he looked at her. "She's a tough nut to crack, but I finally wore her down." He crouched in front of the girls. "And who are these four little princesses?"

"Monsters more like," Angel said with obvious affection, but Gabe saw something in her eyes that told him she was feeling something different.

"This is Jilly, and her sister, Sarah. And these two here are Clare and Claudia."

"Well, it's nice to meet you girls. I'm Gabe. Are you looking forward to going skating?

There was another chorus of *'yes'* as the girls all grinned and smiled.

"Go sit down and put your skates on, girls. I'll be over in a minute."

Gabe straightened as the girls picked up their skates and hurried over to a bench at the edge of the rink. Considering how close it was to Christmas, he was surprised to see there weren't as many people on the ice as there usually was.

· · ·

"You're good with kids," Dani said to him as she retrieved her skates from the floor, "and I think Claudia might have a little crush on you."

Gabe glanced over at the girls, seeing Claudia look away quickly before glancing back, as she started giggling.

"So, how did you two connect? Last I saw, you were taking our table as we were leaving."

Gabe was about to respond to Dani's question, but Angel beat him to it.

"Yeah, long story, but now I can't seem to get rid of him. He just keeps popping up to irritate me."

Like before, her words were meant to be dismissive, but there was no heat behind them. In fact, she was looking at him strangely right now, and he couldn't figure out what that meant.

"Well, however it happened, I'm glad it did. I've not seen Angel with a guy in a long time."
"Oh, I'm not *with* him," Angel said quickly. "He just turned up at my place, and I couldn't shake him off."
"So, he's been to your place then?"

· · ·

This time, Gabe was quicker than Angel and decided he was going to have a little fun with her.

"Yeah, I went back with her Friday night. She kicked me out the next morning though."
"Oh really?"

Gabe watched as Dani turned to Angel with a curious look on her face, and Angel was glaring at him, shooting daggers with her eyes. He grinned at her and tried to pull off the most innocent look he could.

"What? I did go back with you Friday, and you did kick me out the next morning. Am I lying?"
"Well, no, but it wasn't like you're making it sound."
"So, what was it like?"

It was Dani who asked the question, and Gabe wondered what she would say next.

"I got drunk, he helped me home. He slept on the sofa, we had breakfast the next morning, he left. End of story."
"Huh uh," Dani replied. "If you say so."

Angel rolled her eyes again, and Gabe got the distinct impression she wasn't too happy with his teasing, or her friend's questions. Deciding to give her a break, he turned to Dani.

. . .

"She's right. She had one too many and I helped her home. I stayed the night on the sofa to make sure she was okay and left the next morning."

"Aunt Dani, can we go on the ice yet?"

All three of them turned at the sound of Dani's youngest niece, Jilly's, voice. All four girls were standing with their skates laced up, waiting expectantly for the adults to get their act together. The looks on their faces kick-started the adults as Dani started to lace up her skates and Gabe went over to the stand to get skates for him and Angel.

Less than five minutes later, Gabe was stood on the side of the rink with Angel as Dani and the girls whizzed around on the ice. The daylight was starting to fade, which meant hundreds and hundreds of twinkling fairy lights were now clearly visible around the edge of the rink. They had also been strung in the trees and around the edges of the various vendors stalls.

Gabe could hear Christmas music playing, and he sighed deeply. This was why he loved the season so much. Everyone was out having fun, and the fairy lights and music gave everything a festive atmosphere.

Leaning on the railing with his forearms, he glanced across at Angel. She was staring out onto the ice, watching everyone skate past, but the look on her face was one of sadness.

"Hey, what's wrong?"

"Oh nothing. I didn't want to come here in the first place."

Angel turned and leaned against the railing, folding her arms across her chest. Gabe recognised the defensive stance, and he was torn between leaving her be or trying to find out what was bothering her. He knew he stood a good chance of pissing her off again, but if he was certain about following through on his promise to make her love Christmas again, she was going to have to put up with his questioning.

"It's not nothing. I can see it on your face."

Gabe kept his eyes on her as she slowly turned to face him. After a few seconds, she looked out onto the rink. He followed her eyes, seeing she was watching Dani with Jilly as they skated around, hand in hand.

"My Bobby would have been around the same age as Jilly is now. He would have loved it here."

In an instant, Gabe understood what she was saying, and why she hadn't wanted to come. A place like this would be full of children of all ages. There were dozens of youngsters skating around with family and friends. If fate hadn't dealt her a crappy hand, she would probably be here skating around with her son right now. Instead, she was standing here, watching loads of mothers doing what she herself couldn't.

. . .

"Obviously I never met him, but I'm willing to bet he would have loved it here."

"Yes, he would have done." Angel gave him a watery smile before she continued, "He probably would have spent most of his time sprawled on the ice, but he'd have loved it all the same."

"So why don't we get out there and do some skating. For Bobby?"

Taking a chance, Gabe held out his hand to Angel, who he could see was battling an internal war. If he had to guess, he'd say she wanted to get out there onto the ice, but part of her felt guilty for even thinking about having some fun when her son wasn't there to enjoy it with her.

They stayed there for several minutes. Gabe maintained his position as Angel looked between his outstretched hand and the people enjoying themselves on the ice. He wasn't going to rush her. He knew she needed to do this in her own time, and if she decided she didn't want to go out there, he wouldn't either.

If this girl needed one thing, it was support and understanding. He had a feeling that, apart from Dani, she didn't have many friends, at least not many that knew what she had been through. He knew she probably didn't think of him as a friend, but the more time he spent with her, the more he liked her. He could only hope she would one day feel the same about him.

. . .

Gabe was about to drop his arm when he felt her fingers close around his. He looked up at her, seeing her peering at him. She looked almost scared, but she took a deep breath and nodded.

"Let's do this. For Bobby."

He nodded back at her and moved around the railing so he could step onto the ice. There was a slight hesitation, but she followed him, and within moments they were skating around with everyone else that had come out to enjoy the ice rink. When they went past Dani, he saw her watching them, complete with open mouth and look of shock.

After an hour, Gabe and Angel skated over to the edge of the rink and grabbed onto the side. He could see there was a huge smile on her face, and she had spent the last ten minutes laughing as she'd played with the girls. Dani had told him that she came with them to the rink every year, but this year was the first time she'd actually gone on the ice with them, and that was down to him.

Dani had almost been in tears as she hugged him, thanking him over and over for giving her a brief glimpse of the way her friend used to be. Gabe knew they were headed in the right direction, he just hoped they could continue that way, and that Angel didn't start moving backwards after today was over.

CHAPTER
TEN

ANGEL HAD to admit she was having fun. She hadn't thought she would; in fact, she had left her flat that morning determined not to. What she hadn't planned on was Gabe sticking his oar in again, only this time, she was happy he had.

She'd been here with Dani and the girls every year since the fire, but she had always stood on the sidelines, watching, and wondering what it would be like if Bobby was there. She had thought today would be the same, but the moment Gabe held his hand out to her, offering his support to a girl he hardly knew, something inside her had told her to give it a chance. To give him a chance.

Once she was out on the ice with him, he had held onto her hand until she had been ready to go off on her own, and when she did, part of her had felt free. She had skated right up to the girls and grabbed them all from behind, leaving the five of them a laughing heap in the middle of the ice.

She was pretty sure Dani was in shock, as she had just stood there, open-mouthed, while she skated around with the kids, Gabe not too far behind them. He had also joined in the fun, pretending to figure skate with Claudia, who, as Dani had said, clearly had a huge crush on Gabe, and then lifting Jilly up onto his shoulders as she'd squealed with delight.

Gabe.

She found it hard to believe that she was only now learning his name. For all she knew, he'd told her Friday night, but she'd been so far gone she was surprised she remembered her own name, let alone his. She guessed it was short for Gabriel, and if that were true, didn't that make them a weird pairing. Angel and Gabriel. You couldn't get more Christmassy if you tried.

"Are you having fun?"

She turned to Gabe, who was breathing just as quickly as she was, and he had a huge grin on his face. Normally, she would say yes just to keep people happy, but right now, she could say yes and really mean it.

"Thank you for making me get out there today. I needed someone to talk me into it. Dani has never succeeded. I don't know why I let you convince me."

"I guess I just have a knack with words."

He smiled at her warmly, a smile she returned, and this time it was genuine. They stood there for several moments just looking at each other, and Angel felt her pulse begin to quicken again, only this time it had nothing to do with skating and everything to do with the man who stood less than a foot away from her.

"Incoming!"

Angel heard the shout from Dani and turned, just as Jilly and Sarah came barrelling into her. If it hadn't been for Gabe being so close, she'd have tumbled into a pile on the floor with the girls. As it was, he'd grabbed hold of her waist, keeping her upright as the girls dissolved into fits of giggles on the ice in front of her.

Her back was pressed up against his chest, and the warmth of his body spread through hers. It had been too long since she had been this close to a man, even if it was only because he had stopped her from falling. Yet she was safely on her feet, and his hands still gripped her waist tightly.

"Are you okay?" Gabe asked, his warm breath fanning across her face as he leaned forward and angled his head so he could see her.

Was she okay? She wasn't entirely sure. Her proximity to him was causing her insides to tremble, and her whole body felt like it was overheating. Her brain knew he was asking her if she was okay following the collision with the girls, but her body was telling her otherwise, and right now, she didn't want to listen to her head.

"No. Not really."

Angel felt his hands tighten at her waist as his eyes darkened, and she knew she wasn't the only one who felt it. Something was happening between them, despite her initial resistance. When her gaze flicked down to his lips, he licked them slowly, and she felt her stomach flip-flop at the simple action.

Unless she was imagining it, his face was getting closer to hers. She wanted him to kiss her. Even though they were in public, with Dani somewhere around, she found she didn't care. In that moment, she wanted to feel his lips on hers, if only for a brief moment.

"Angel?"

The sound of her voice was like someone throwing a bucket of cold water over her. She turned away from Gabe, but he still held her against him. When she saw who had called her name, she went stock still.

She had never met the woman that stood in front of her, but she would know her anywhere. The tall brunette had scars on the left side of her face, scars that went down her neck and vanished into the top of her winter coat. Her left eye was partially closed, and her hair had been fixed so it didn't show the patches she knew were there.

"Donna?"

The sole survivor of the fire that killed her entire family stood in front of her, and she had no clue what to say. This was a woman who might be able to tell her things about the day of the fire, but she had never found the courage to ask.

"It's okay. I'm here."

She heard Gabe whisper in her ear, and she was suddenly grateful he was there, if for no other reason than she couldn't run if he was holding her, which he still was. She hadn't told Gabe her name, so guessed he had figured out who she was by her appearance. The fact he wanted to support her through this meeting, after less than forty-eight hours of knowing her, spoke volumes about the kind of man he was.

"How are you? I've tried getting in touch, but I guess it was still too raw for you."

"I'm okay," Angel replied quietly. "It still hurts, every day, but I guess it will always be that way."

Angel watched as Donna just nodded, then a guy walked up and stood next to her. He was a few inches taller than she was, with dirty blonde hair down to his shoulders. He was wrapped up in a thick Parka, with a scarf around his neck.

"Hey, babe, everything okay?"

"Oh, Matt, this is Angel. She's Andy's sister."

Angel saw his face change immediately, and she recognised it for what it was. Pity. This man, who she had never met before, who clearly knew about her brother and what had happened, pitied her. As if a switch had been flipped, Angel was back in that hospital waiting room, and she could feel the tears burning behind her eyes.

"I've got you. You're okay."

"No, I need to get out of here. I need to go."

Angel forced herself out of Gabe's hold and pushed past Donna and her friend. After removing her skates, she left them in a heap on the floor as she pulled on her boots. Within a few minutes, she was rushing through the carpark and heard gravel crunching behind her, knowing instantly who it was.

"Leave me alone, Gabe."

"I'm not leaving you when you're this upset. I drove remember?" Gabe said as he shook his keys in his hand.

"I can take the bus."

"The hell you will," Gabe exclaimed as he took her arm, bringing her to a stop. "You're upset, and you're shaking like a leaf. Now, I'm driving you home, and I won't argue with you, Angel. Now get your butt over to my car right now, or I'll carry you there."

Angel huffed out a breath. "You wouldn't dare."

"Try me."

Angel looked at him, trying to decide whether she wanted to risk calling his bluff, only to then be royally embarrassed if he actually did pick her up and carry her to his car.

"Fine."

"Good. Now, was that so hard?"

Gabe unlocked the car when she reached it, and she climbed into the passenger seat. After fastening her seatbelt, she closed her eyes and leaned back against the headrest. She didn't want to talk right now. She just wanted to sit here and think about anything other than what had just happened.

She heard the door open and close as he got in the driver's side, followed by the click of his seatbelt. There was silence for a few moments, and Angel figured he was watching her, trying to think of something to say. She was grateful when he didn't say anything. He just started the engine, and they pulled away.

The fifteen-minute drive back to her place was done in silence. When the car slowed to a stop and the engine went quiet, Angel opened her eyes and unbuckled her seatbelt, avoiding eye contact with Gabe as she went to open the car door. She stopped when she felt his hand on her arm.

"Don't run from me, Angel. Please."

His voice was almost pleading with her, and she felt bad that she had been planning on doing just that. She risked turning to him, regretting it immediately when she saw the look in his eyes.

"I'm not. I just want to get inside."

"Okay. Can I come up too? We haven't eaten today. I figured we could get pizza? You don't have to talk if you don't want to. I won't push. We can just watch crappy TV and put the world to rights. What do you say?"

Angel pondered his request for all of a few seconds before deciding what she wanted to do. She didn't want to talk about what had happened with Donna because she knew it would only result in a snotty tear fest, something she didn't want to do in front of him. But there was something she wanted to talk about.

They'd had a moment at the ice rink, and it confused her. No matter how much she didn't want to be, she was attracted to Gabe. Seeing the way he had interacted with Dani's nieces today had made her insides clench, and she was sure her ovaries had exploded.

Having kids again after losing Bobby had never crossed her mind. In fact, she tried to avoid children altogether, knowing they would only remind her of what she no longer had. Yet seeing Gabe with the girls today had made her rethink her stance on children. She was by no means ready to have another child, but the idea wasn't completely out of the question now.

She knew, just from those few moments, that Gabe would be a great father. She also knew that thinking of him as the father to her possible future children was ridiculous, as nothing even close to sex had happened between them. But they'd still had that moment, and she wanted to explore that further.

"Okay, but you're buying."

The grin Gabe gave her told her he was pleased with her

answer as he turned to open the door and climb out. Less than five minutes later, they were in her flat and he was on his phone ordering one super large pepperoni pizza with extra onions and mushrooms.

While he was doing that, she went through to her bedroom and grabbed a pair of jogging bottoms and an old Bon Jovi tour t-shirt from her wardrobe. She quickly changed, and she didn't know why, but she checked her appearance in the mirror before heading back out to find him sat in the corner of her sofa.

"Pizza will be here in twenty."

"Great. Can I get you a drink? Tea, coffee or something stronger?"

"I'd love something stronger, but I have to drive so I'll stick with tea."

Angel nodded and moved into the kitchen, filling the kettle and prepping the mugs.

"You don't need to have tea just because I am. Have a glass of wine if you want."

Angel jumped at the sound of his voice, turning to see him standing right behind her. How had he gotten there without her hearing him? She looked up at him to see him watching her. His head was tilted slightly, and unless she was imagining it, he was moving closer.

"What are you doing?" she asked quietly, suddenly aware that her voice was a whisper the nearer he got.

"We started something earlier. I need to finish it."

With those words, his mouth came down on hers. The contact took her by surprise, and she was torn between grabbing hold of him and throwing herself into the kiss or maintaining her position by the counter. When she felt his tongue run across the seam of her mouth, she moaned, and he took advantage, pushing his tongue past her lips as his hands gripped her hips, holding her still.

She stroked his tongue with her own and let him hold her,

feeling his erection against her stomach. That was all it took for Angel to throw caution to the wind and throw her arms around his neck. Before she knew what was happening, he had lifted her up, and she was now sat on the countertop. The new height made it easier for her to meet his kiss as she wiggled forward, whimpering when she felt his hard length between her legs.

Had he read her mind? She'd invited him up with the intention of exploring what had almost happened between them earlier, but her plan had been to talk about it, to see where they both stood. She'd be lying if she said kissing Gabe hadn't crossed her mind, because it had, dozens of times, and good God the man could kiss.

Angel continued to hold onto him as his hands flexed on her thighs. She felt him slow the kiss before he pulled away, but he stayed standing between her thighs as he looked at her.

"Thought so," he said, a little breathless.

"You thought what?"

"That we had a moment earlier. Didn't think I'd imagined it."

"You didn't. I felt it too."

Angel smiled as his hands slid under her thighs and he lifted her from the counter, allowing her to slide down his body. Her blood was still coursing through her veins; her heart still beating a rapid rhythm as her feet reconnected with the floor. She released her hands from around his neck and slid them down to rest on his upper arms. She couldn't resist a little squeeze of his biceps, and in return he lowered his hands from her hips to squeeze her butt.

They stood there for several moments, just looking at each other, when a knock on the door broke the spell. She saw Gabe furrow his brow at the interruption, before he realised it was the pizza he'd ordered not too long ago. Giving her butt one last squeeze, he released her and headed over to the front door while Angel turned and finished the drinks she'd started earlier.

She had thought having the conversation about their 'moment' would be awkward, but now that he had broken the ice by kissing her, it might not be so bad.

CHAPTER ELEVEN

AS HE SAT on the sofa with Angel, eating pizza and watching whatever reality TV show she had put on, he still had no idea what had gotten into him.

Gabe hadn't planned on kissing her tonight. The only thing he had planned on was keeping her company and stopping her from dwelling over whatever had gone on at the ice rink to make her dash out of there so quickly.

He knew seeing Donna had been a shock. He had felt the change in her as soon as she saw her. Her body went tense, and she had started shaking. It hadn't taken much guesswork on his part to figure out who the woman was. She may have survived the fire three years ago, but it had left her with scars that even makeup couldn't cover.

"Can I ask you a question?"

. . .

He watched as Angel looked at him, before crossing her legs and giving him her full attention. At least she seemed more comfortable around him, and she wasn't batting away his questions.

"Shoot."

"Earlier today, when that guy, Matt, came over, what made you run? You seemed to be okay talking with Donna. I was just wondering what changed."

He half expected her to build her walls again, to refuse to answer his question and ask him to leave, so he was surprised when she just took a breath and started talking.

"After the fire, I was in a bad way. I don't think I left the house for five, maybe six weeks. The only one I would let through that door was Dani, and that's only because she was with me at the hospital when they told me what had happened. When I did eventually pluck up the nerve to leave the house, I was sure everyone knew. They were all looking at me and whispering as I went past. They weren't even trying to hide it. A few people, mainly neighbours or friends of the family, came up to me to express their sympathies, but the look on everyone's face was the same. Pity. I didn't want to be pitied, and I still don't. Whenever anyone realises who I am, or finds out what happened, they pity me. That guy, Matt, did exactly the same thing, and when he did, I was right back in that hospital. I needed to get out of there."

"I'm so sorry. I didn't realise."

"Why would you?" she said with a shrug. "You weren't there to see the faces of all those people over the years. You wouldn't have known any different." Angel took a breath, and to his surprise, reached out and took his hand. "You know, you're the only one who didn't give me that look of pity when I told you what happened. I was expecting the same from you that I've had from everyone else. I'd prepared myself for it, but it never happened. Why is that? Why were you different from everyone else?"

"I had similar responses from people when they found out about what Gemma did to our baby. I hated it too. There's a thin line between sympathy and pity, and I always try and make sure never to cross it. That, and with what little I know of you, I figured you wouldn't appreciate it. Guess I was right."

Gabe smiled at her and squeezed her hand that still held onto his. She gave him a small nod before turning back to the TV, just as his phone chirped to indicate a message. He picked it up and opened the little envelope:

How are you doing, Gabe? Looks like you had a lovely time at the ice rink today. Blondie, too, until that guy upset her. She seems like a sensitive sort, that one. I'd be careful. One foot wrong and she'll be sobbing all over the place. Trust me, I know the type. Oh, and what was going on with that chick with all the scars? Weirdo. Anyway, you looking for some action tonight? Think she'll let you get under the covers again? You might need to get her pissed first though, looks like a frigid one that. Cool car, by the way. Dying to know how you manage to afford that. Gotta go. Bye for now."

Gabe read the message again before pulling his hand from Angel's and hurrying over to the window. He gazed out onto the street and saw no one who looked familiar. What the hell was she playing at? It had been years since they'd seen each other, let alone spoken to each other.

He inwardly cursed himself for responding to her message the other day. He had opened the floodgates, and he knew these messages wouldn't stop anytime soon. Gemma had never been the possessive sort when they were together, but she was starting to sound like it now.

"Hey, what's wrong?"

Gabe turned to see Angel standing behind him, trying to look out the window with him. Her hand was resting against his back as she rose on tiptoes to try and see around him. As Gabe looked down at her, he felt an overwhelming need to protect her, which was stupid, seeing as he had known her less than forty-eight hours. What had this girl done to him?

"Oh, nothing. I thought I heard something, that's all. Must be my imagination."

He forced himself to turn away from the window as she took a step back, so she was in front of him.

"You sure you don't want something stronger than tea?" she asked him, looking away briefly. "You don't have to go home tonight if you don't want to. What I mean to say is, I would like the company."

· · ·

She looked nervous as she spoke, and something told him she didn't normally ask guys to stay the night. Was he the first? Truth be told, he had thought about asking if he could stay, on the sofa of course. Even now, he didn't want to assume he would be spending the night in her bed. While another night on that sofa wouldn't be his first choice, if it meant being close to her, he would take it. When he added in the concerns he had about Gemma's apparent interest in her, staying over was probably going to be the only way he would sleep tonight.

"Sure, I'd like that."

She gave him a shy smile before moving over to the fridge. After opening the door, she reached in with both hands and brought out two bottles.

"I have wine, beer or…" she put down the wine and opened the freezer to bring out another bottle, "vodka."
"I'll take a beer, please."

She nodded and placed the wine on the counter before diving back into the fridge, bringing out yet another bottle.

"Corona or Bud?"

He pondered his choices before reaching out and taking the bottle in her left hand. She smiled as she put the Corona back in the fridge and the vodka in the freezer, before grabbing a corkscrew out of one of the drawers so she could open the wine.

Gabe watched her move around her kitchen as he opened his Bud and leaned against the counter. When she had poured her wine, she put the bottle back in the fridge and started to walk back into the living room. He carried on watching her, smiling when she stopped and turned to him.

"You coming, or are you going to stand there looking at me all night?"

"If it's all the same to you, I'll keep looking at you."

When she rolled her eyes at him and sat on the sofa, he let out a small laugh, before he joined her. There were two slices of pizza left in the box, so they both reached out and grabbed one each before sitting back to continue watching TV.

This was nice. He hadn't felt this comfortable around a woman in a long time, and this woman he'd known for such a short time. He still wasn't sure what it was about her that kept him coming back. He knew it was curiosity that initially made him want to speak with her, but what kept him interested?

He could say it was because she was so damn beautiful, but that wasn't the reason. Sure, it was a nice side benefit, but he had never been that superficial. At least, he didn't think he had. It was her vulnerability that attracted him. She came across to most people as a strong woman, especially with everything she had been through, but now that he knew her a bit better, he knew otherwise.

Here was a woman who struggled to let go of the demons from her past. A woman who, after three years, still couldn't move on from the tragedy that had taken away her family. So much so that she hated a time of year that was meant to be full of joy and hope.

Gabe took a swig of his beer as he polished off his slice of pizza, groaning as she flipped the channel to yet another reality show. She turned her head at the sound of his grumble and threw him a look.

"What?"
"Is there something on that's not going to kill off my brain cells? I think my IQ has dropped ten points since we got back."

After giving him a look that could stop traffic, she picked up her now empty wine glass and tossed him the remote control.

"Fine, if you're not happy with my choices, you find something. I'm going to get a refill. Do you want another?"
"Please."

Gabe finished the rest of his beer and handed her the empty bottle before switching his attention to the TV. He didn't care what he watched, as long as it wasn't anything to do with celebrities learning to dance, ice skate, being stuck in a jungle eating crap he didn't even want to think of, or in a huge-ass house with everyone watching their every move. He'd rather watch the soaps than any of that. Actually, come to think of it, maybe not.

When he got to a movie channel, he checked the guide, seeing what movie was about to start. Whilst it wouldn't normally be his first choice, he had yet to meet a woman who didn't like this film. Tonight was all about keeping Angel's mind off what had happened today. If it meant he had to sit through a film he wasn't one hundred percent on board with, he would tolerate it if she was happy.

He put the remote control back on the sofa between them just as she came back with another beer for him and her wine glass topped up. He took a swig and put the bottle on the table, as she sat down just as the credits began to roll, and a huge grin spread across her face.

"How did you know I love this movie?"

"Not a big secret. All girls love this movie. Or should I say, all girls love Patrick Swayze."

They smiled at each other before she put her wine down, shifted across the sofa, and placed a soft kiss to his lips. It took him by surprise, but he let her continue. She only held it for several seconds, but when she broke away, his lips tingled from her touch, and he felt the kiss was all too brief.

. . .

When she went to move away, Gabe decided he wasn't ready for her to shift back over to the other end of the sofa, so his hands snaked out and took hold of her arms, pulling her back towards him.

The movement took her by surprise, and she tumbled forward. Her hands pressed into his chest, and when she lifted her head to look at him, there was a huge smile on her face. Seeing that she wasn't upset with his actions, Gabe wasted no time in crushing his lips to hers, spurred on by the moan that passed her lips as her body aligned with his on the sofa.

This time it was her tongue that sought entry, which he willingly granted as his arms banded around her back, preventing her from moving even if she wanted to. His tongue stroked hers as the temperature in the room soared. Everything started to fade away, and all he could concentrate on was the woman in his arms and the sensations flooding his body.

He wanted nothing more than to strip them both naked, flip her onto her back and bury himself inside her, but he knew that would be moving too quickly, no matter how much his body was begging for release. If they were going to go to that stage, she needed to be the one to initiate it. He wasn't going to rush her into something she may not be ready for.

After a few minutes, Angel broke the kiss and pulled away. Gabe was about to reach out for her and tug her back, but she shifted position and straddled his lap. When her hands wound around his neck and she kissed him again, he thought he may have to rethink his earlier idea of her being the initiator, especially when she scooted forward and settled over his already hard length.

He held her close as they kissed for several minutes, his fingers tugging on the band that held her hair in a ponytail. With it gone, her blonde hair spilled over her shoulders, and he broke the kiss and gently pushed her back.

He looked at her as if seeing her for the first time; slightly parted lips that were swollen from their kisses, flushed cheeks, cascading hair. In that moment, Gabe was sure his heart had stopped beating as he thought she definitely lived up to her name.

"God, you look beautiful."

The smile she gave him kickstarted his heart again as she stood and held her hand out to him. He took it and rose from the sofa, letting her lead him through to the bedroom, flipping off lights as she went. When they fell onto the bed, a tangle of arms and legs, Gabe missed the text that lit up his phone. A text which read:

Sleep tight.

CHAPTER
TWELVE

ANGEL AWOKE THE NEXT MORNING, realising immediately that she wasn't alone. She was pressed into the mattress by an arm banded across her stomach, a head on her shoulder, and two legs tangled with hers. She was so hot she felt like she might pass out any minute, but she wouldn't be anywhere else.

She smiled as she recalled what had happened last night, as she remembered that Gabe had been the perfect gentleman. They'd kissed until they were breathless, and she'd gotten another glimpse of that near perfect torso. They touched and stroked each other until they'd explored every inch of flesh, and then Gabe had put the brakes on.

To say she'd been disappointed would be an understatement, but when he'd explained that tonight, he just wanted to lie with her and be close to her, any disappointment washed away. He had wrapped her in his shirt and pulled her to him. She recalled falling asleep to the steady sound of his heartbeat and the gentle pull of his fingers running through her hair.

Angel couldn't remember a time when she had slept so peacefully. There was no restlessness or any bad dreams. She'd woken at around 2am in the same position she'd been four hours earlier. Gabe's arms were wrapped tightly around her, and their legs were wound together under the covers. She'd just sighed and relaxed into his hold.

Now, it was almost 8am. He was still wrapped around her like a blanket, and she really needed to pee. Angel lifted his arm and tried to unravel her legs from his, but she soon figured out it wasn't going to be as easy as she'd hoped. As her bladder started to protest, she was close to just shoving him off her, when she heard a mumble.

"Comfy. Warm. Keep still."

His arm tightened around her waist as he pulled her closer, his face pressing into the skin of her neck as he breathed deeply.

"Mmm, smell good."

When he started kissing her neck, Angel was tempted to just lie there and let him continue, but if she didn't get up now, she'd have an accident that she was sure he would never let her live down.

"Hold that thought."

After extricating herself from his hold, Angel moved as fast as she could to the bathroom to relieve herself. When she returned, the sight that greeted her was definitely something she could get used to. He'd shifted position so he was now sitting up against the pillows. The sheets were pulled up to his waist, and one arm was resting behind his head, giving her an unobstructed view of his impressive abs.

The first thought that jumped into her head was how sexy he looked. The second was how much she wanted to climb on top of him and have her way until they were both too exhausted to move. When he turned his head to look at her, the smile he gave her made her belly flip flop as she rounded the bed, climbed in next to him, and cuddled into his chest.

His arms fell around her shoulders as her eyes closed. She could very easily go back to sleep right now. All she had to do was relax and absorb the warmth coming from his body.

"My shirt looks good on you," he said, causing Angel to smile into his chest as she lifted her head to look at him. "What do you want to do today?"

"I'm more than happy to stay here," Angel said as she burrowed back into his chest.

"Well, as appealing as that sounds, I have things I need to do. Christmas is only four days away, and I've not done any shopping. You can come with me if you like? A woman's point of view is always welcome."

Angel sighed at his words and sat up, causing his arm to fall from her shoulders. She'd been wondering when he would try and get her to do something Christmassy again. She had pushed it to the back of her mind after the good time they'd had yesterday, but it had never been too far away. After all, he did promise he would make it his mission to make her enjoy Christmas again.

"Actually, I have things to do too. Why don't you go, do your shopping, and I'll see you later maybe, or tomorrow, or whenever."

She went to get out of bed when he reached out and took her arm.

"I'd rather do it with you, Angel. You know, you might even enjoy it once we get out there amongst all the other shoppers."

"Don't tell me what I will and won't enjoy," Angel said as she pulled her arm from his grasp and stood. She grabbed her jogging bottoms before pulling them on. "You know I don't like shopping, especially at Christmas, so don't push me."

Angel scooped up her discarded t-shirt and stomped into the bathroom, closing the door. She had a feeling he would follow her, so she slid the lock across and sat on the edge of the bath.

Why did he have to go and ruin everything? They'd had a lovely evening, and the morning wasn't going too badly either, until he had to open his mouth. She'd told him she wasn't interested in Christmas shopping, but still he pushed. Why couldn't he just take no for an answer?

"Angel? Please, come out. I'm sorry."

Just hearing his voice was making her angry as she stripped off his shirt and tugged her t-shirt over her head. Unlocking the door, she opened it, flung his shirt at him, and closed it again.

"Get lost, Gabe. Go do your shopping. Maybe I'll see you around sometime."

She placed her hand on the door and leaned forward, resting her forehead against the wood. There was silence for several minutes before she heard him start to move around. It was a full ten minutes before she heard her front door open and close, and she stepped out of the bathroom.

Angel saw that her bed was made, and what remained of the clothes she had discarded the night before were on a nearby chair. There was also a note on her bedside table. Walking over, she sat on the edge of the bed she had been lying in with Gabe only thirty minutes ago. She picked up the paper, and began to read:

Angel,

I'm sorry if I upset you. That was the last thing I wanted to do. I just thought that after the fun you had at the ice rink yesterday… actually, I don't know what I thought. All I know is that we had a fun day—well, most of it—followed by a lovely evening, and I thought we could continue that today.

Waking up to you this morning was unlike anything I've felt in a long time. I woke several times last night to find you wrapped around me. I can't tell you how hard it was not to wake you up and continue where we left off before we settled for the night.

You're a curious and intriguing woman, Angel, and I hope I've not pushed too hard too quickly. I know you need to do this in your own time, and it was stupid of me not to listen when you told me you weren't interested in shopping.

I've left my number at the bottom. I shall leave it to you to decide if you want to see me again. I hope you will, and that I'll hear from you soon.

Gabe

Angel put the paper on the bed beside her and swiped at the tear that was threatening to fall. How could one man piss her off one minute, then almost reduce her to tears the next? She didn't even know why she was upset. The old Angel would just chalk him up to another bad choice in men and move on. As far as she was concerned, she hadn't changed, so why was this particular guy getting under her skin?

CHAPTER
THIRTEEN

WHY HAD HE PUSHED HER? Why couldn't he have just accepted that she didn't want to go shopping and suggest something else for them to do? Now, he had no way of keeping her safe.

Maybe he should have just told her the truth? Explained to her that he thought someone might be out to get her as a way to get at him. Yeah, if he did that, she would think he was crazy, even certifiable, and he definitely wouldn't get to see her again.

She had fallen asleep before him last night, and he'd seen the message on his phone. He'd known who it would be from. No one else would text him at that time of night. He'd also known the timing of the message had coincided with when they'd gone to bed and switched the lights out.

Gabe had also woken before her that morning and seen another message, congratulating him on not getting kicked out. The only way she would know any of these things would be if she had been outside Angel's flat last night to see the place fall into darkness, and then saw his car still parked there this morning.

He wasn't at the panic stage yet, but he hadn't seen

Gemma in a long time. He didn't know the woman she was now, or what she was capable of. There was a good chance she was just playing him up, trying to cause trouble for him, and had no intention of doing anything to Angel. However, the fact that she seemed to be following one, or both, of them raised several red flags in his eyes, and he wasn't about to let anything happen to Angel.

Gabe had originally planned on just leaving her place like she had asked, but he decided to leave the note at the last minute. He'd added his phone number as an afterthought. He hoped she would get in touch, and that he hadn't pushed her too far. She'd been pretty adamant about him going, which was why he'd done just that and not tried to talk her into letting him stay.

All Gabe could do now was wait and pray that she called him. Then again, if she knew he was parked down the street, just far enough away that she wouldn't see him if she looked out, yet close enough that he could see if anyone was watching her, she would probably kick him to the kerb permanently.

He had been here for three hours so far. His stomach was growling, and his back was killing him. Comfortable the seats might be when driving, but they weren't designed for prolonged periods of slouching down to avoid being seen by passers-by. Gabe knew he couldn't stay out here forever. All he could do now was hope she got in touch with him, that he hadn't completely blown his chances.

Sitting up in his seat, he winced at the twinge in his back as he pushed the key into the ignition. Checking his mirrors, Gabe pulled away. The traffic was light, and he figured it would only take him ten minutes to get home. When he got there, and he was comfortable, he could try and figure out what he could do to get back in Angel's good books. He wasn't in the mood for Christmas shopping anymore, even though he knew he needed to get it done eventually.

When he reached the end of her street and flicked on his indicator to turn left, his eyes landed on the car waiting to turn right, specifically the driver. He knew those eyes. He'd once gazed into them while in the throes of passion. She'd been a blonde when he'd known her, now she was a redhead. She looked different, but it was her. He was sure of it.

When the car to his right flashed his lights, Gabe was frozen on the spot as her car moved forward, entering the street he was about to leave. She glanced across, giving him a small wave as she went by. The car behind honked it's horn, and Gabe had no choice but to continue on.

He knew when he eventually got to turn around, she would be gone. Had she been going that way to see if he was still there? Or had she simply been turning onto the road to get wherever she had been going? Gabe knew he was beginning to sound a little paranoid, but after the texts she had sent him, he didn't think he could afford not to be, not if Angel's safety could be at risk.

He travelled a short distance down the road until he came to a spot in which he could turn. Within moments, he was turning back onto Angel's street, and he slowed the car, making sure to look at each car that was parked, but none of them were the one Gemma had been driving.

Maybe, knowing he wasn't at Angel's place anymore, she'd just carried on to wherever she had been going. At least he now knew what she looked like, and what she drove. It would make it easier for him to keep an eye open for her.

Gabe glanced towards Angel's flat as he went past, seeing her standing by the window. She was on the phone, her hand flying around as she spoke. Whoever she was speaking to, it looked like she was arguing with them.

He slowed to a stop and just watched her. When she ended the call, he saw her fling her phone across the room, then bury her face in her hands. He didn't need to see her face to know she was crying, but he didn't know if it was out of anger or if she was upset about something.

Gabe was so tempted to jump out the car, race to her front door, and make sure she was okay, but he didn't. He just sat there, his heart breaking a little as her shoulders shook with her sobs. When she looked up, it was as if her eyes were drawn to him as they connected with his.

She held his stare for several moments, before she turned away and vanished from his view. Gabe didn't know what to do. After the way they'd left things earlier, he didn't think she would want him back in her place just yet, but he couldn't just drive off and leave her when something was clearly wrong. He took a deep breath and hit his fist against the steering wheel in frustration. He was about to drive off, when there was a knock on the side window, and he saw Angel looking at him.

He opened the window, and she said four words before turning to go back inside.

"We need to talk."

CHAPTER
FOURTEEN

ANGEL FOLDED her arms and crossed the street, heading back towards the building that housed her flat. She knew he was behind her; she had heard the car door slam, then his footsteps a few paces behind her.

She'd planned on calling him to tell him to get his arse there asap, but when she'd looked up and seen him sat outside her place, she hadn't been sure whether to be happy he was there, as it saved her a phone call, or pissed that he appeared to be spying on her, and knowing what she knew now, wouldn't that be a kick in the teeth.

Opening the main door, she didn't hold it open for him as she walked down the hallway and got to her front door. Before she got it open, she could feel him standing behind her. He'd not said anything to her yet, probably because he didn't know what to say.

. . .

She'd be willing to bet he hadn't planned on her coming down to see him. She hadn't planned it herself, but after that phone call, then seeing him outside, she needed some answers, and she wasn't prepared to wait for them.

Angel pushed open the door, letting him follow her in. When she reached the living room, she took a breath before she turned on him.

"Why the fuck am I getting calls from your clearly psycho ex-girlfriend?"

The look on his face wasn't what Angel had been expecting nor hoping for. She'd wanted to see shock and surprise, but what she saw was more like resignation.

"You knew?"
"No… Yes—no. What I mean is, I didn't know she was going to contact you. I thought she was just playing with me."
"Playing with you how? What haven't you been telling me?"

Angel was trying to stay calm, but so far, she was failing miserably. Since she had asked him to leave that morning, she'd done nothing but mope around her flat, eating junk food and drinking copious amounts of coffee. The latter could explain why she felt so amped up now.

"Spit it out, Gabe, because I know you're hiding something."

. . .

She watched him run his hands through his hair before letting his hands fall to his sides.

"Can we sit down? If I'm going to tell you this, I'd rather be sitting."

Angel waved her hand in the direction of the sofa. "And I'd like coffee," she said as she walked to the kitchen, coming back several minutes later with two mugs. She handed one to him then sat at the far end of the sofa, turning so she could look at him square on. "So? What the hell is going on?"

"It's probably easier if I show you first, then explain."

She watched as he pulled his phone out of his pocket. After unlocking it with his thumbprint, he scrolled through a few menus before handing the device to her. She saw that they were text messages. The number that sent them had no name attached to it, meaning it wasn't a number he had in his contacts.

Angel read each text in turn, her blood turning cold as she did so. There were only three messages, but they made it clear that she was being watched by the woman Gabe had told her about the first time he'd been around there; the woman who had aborted his—their unborn baby.

. . .

"You told me you hadn't heard from her in years. Why has she decided to contact you now, and why the hell is she stalking me?"

"It's not you she's stalking, it's me."

"Oh, that makes it all right then," Angel replied sarcastically. "It doesn't matter who she is stalking, she's all but made threats against me. Should I be worried? Why did she contact you after so long?"

Angel watched as Gabe sipped at his coffee, and she believed he was stalling for time so he could figure out how to answer her questions.

"I get a message from her every few months. Usually I just ignore them. I've been doing that for years. But for some reason, when I got the first message the other night, I replied, and as you can see, it went from there. I don't remember her being vicious, but when she replied to me that first time, it was clear she'd been at the bar and probably followed us back here afterwards. I don't know if she followed me to the bar earlier in the evening, or if it was just coincidence she was there, but then I saw her earlier—"

"Wait? You saw her earlier? Is that why you were outside? God, is that why you keep coming back here? Just because of her?"

Now he did look shocked, but why, she wasn't sure.

"What? No, of course not. Well, not all of that."

"What bits, exactly, because I have to tell you, Gabe, I'm all sorts of confused right now."

"Okay. Yes, I saw her earlier, and yes, that's why I was outside when you saw me. But no, she isn't why I keep coming back here. I keep coming back, because believe it or not, Angel, I like you, and I want to spend time with you." He put his coffee on the table and moved closer to her, but he didn't touch her. "Think about it. I didn't get the first message from her until after I met you in the bar. It was also after I stayed over, and after we enjoyed a nice breakfast. I knew then that I wanted to get to know you better, so when I pushed too hard and you kicked me out, I felt like crap. That night, I just laid in bed going over everything I had messed up, and her message came through. I had a 'what the hell' moment and replied, which I'm now regretting."

Angel listened to his words, not sure whether he meant what he was saying or if he was saying it just to avoid pissing her off again. There was a part of her that wanted to believe he enjoyed spending time with her, and that was the reason he kept showing up, but there was another part of her that thought differently.

Gabe was a good-looking guy, who, if he was so inclined, could get any girl he wanted, and she had never been the kind of girl that guys went after in that way.

"So, what you're saying is that if I hadn't kicked you out, you wouldn't have felt like crap, wouldn't have responded to her text, and none of this would be happening. So all this is my fault somehow?"

"Now you're twisting what I'm saying, Angel. I have never thought of it that way, and I must admit, I'm a little shocked that your mind went in that direction. I thought we were getting somewhere, until what happened this morning. Or did I imagine everything that's gone on since Friday night?"

She couldn't lie to him. He hadn't imagined it. She thought they were getting somewhere too, but with his need for her to love Christmas—something she couldn't ever see happening again—and his batshit crazy, stalker ex-girlfriend, she couldn't see how it could work between them.

"No, you weren't imagining things, but that was then. This is now, Gabe, and you want something I just can't give you, and it's clear Gemma is going to be an issue if she's sending you messages like this every time we see each other. I think it's best if we just call it quits. You go your way, and I'll go mine."

She held out his phone, and when he took it, Angel stood and walked over to the front door.

"Not going to happen, Angel," Gabe said forcefully. "I'm not letting you kick me out again. Not until we've sorted this out."

"It's sorted, Gabe. We want different things, and—"

"Bullshit," he responded as he stood. "You're scared. You're scared of having a good time, of enjoying your life, of enjoying Christmas, because somewhere in that head of yours, a little voice is telling you that you shouldn't. Well, I'm telling you that it's all bullshit, Angel. What happened to your family, it was a tragic accident, but you can't live your life like this." She saw the hesitation before he continued, "You can't go on blaming yourself."

"He shouldn't have been there," Angel whispered, so quietly she knew he didn't hear her.

"It's not your fault, Angel."

This time she didn't whisper, she screamed, "He shouldn't have been there! It's my fault he's dead!"

No matter how much she tried to hold them back, she couldn't stop the tears falling down her cheeks. Soon, they were coming thick and fast, and before she knew it, Gabe's arms were wrapped around her, and she was clinging to him for dear life.

oOo

It had taken her almost twenty minutes to stop crying, five to convince Gabe that she was okay, and another ten to wash up and feel remotely human again. Now, she had a distinct feeling of déjà vu as they sat at opposite ends of the sofa and she prepared to tell him something she had never told anyone.

"I'd been so busy at work that I hadn't done any of my Christmas shopping. I never usually leave it to the last minute, but I wanted to make as much money as I could so I could give Bobby a great Christmas. That meant working weekends and often late into the evening, so Christmas Eve was the only day I had to get the presents. As Mum and Dad were having lunch with Andy and Donna, Bobby was meant to be coming with me." Her voice cracked as she spoke about her baby boy, but she was determined to make him understand what she had meant by her earlier statement, and why this time of year was so painful for her.

"It was a big thing for Andy. It was the first time he was introducing Donna to Mum and Dad, so he didn't want Bobby in the way." She smiled as she recalled a memory. "Bobby was into everything, so there was no doubt he would disrupt the nice, peaceful lunch Andy and my parents wanted, but I didn't want Bobby with me while I went shopping. It was going to be awkward enough carrying all the bags, but with a buggy and a teething two-year-old, it would be pretty much impossible. I promised Andy I would get him anything he wanted for his birthday if he would do this one thing for me. He really didn't want to, but I had a way of wrapping him around my little finger. We were twins, you know. Most people didn't know because he had such a baby face and looked younger by a few years, but he was my twin."

Angel paused a moment and closed her eyes, taking a few deep breaths. She was determined to get through this without crying, and when she felt Gabe take her hand, she nearly broke, but managed to continue.

"Andy agreed to keep Bobby with him, saying Donna would love to meet him, so I gave him a hug to thank him, kissed and hugged Bobby, then waved to Mum and Dad as I left the house. I went out, did my shopping, and was on my way to meet Dani and a friend for lunch, when the police called me about the fire. Bobby should have been with me. If I had just sucked it up and taken him shopping with me, he would still be alive. Instead, I left him at home while I went out to enjoy myself without him. He should be alive, and he isn't because I was too bloody selfish to take him shopping with me!"

She was crying again now, but she held a hand up to stop Gabe from moving closer. These weren't tears of sadness, these were tears of anger.

"Why the fuck should I enjoy Christmas when I robbed my baby boy of his chance to enjoy it? Why the fuck should I be happy when he will never get the chance to be happy? And why the fuck should I have fun when he isn't here to have fun with me? Answer me that, Gabe. Why the fuck should I do all those things?"

She was practically vibrating with anger as she looked at him, waiting for his answer. When he gave it to her, it wasn't what she expected, and it practically knocked the wind right out of her.

"Because you're alive."

CHAPTER
FIFTEEN

IT WAS ALL SO clear now. Why she hated Christmas. Why she refused to let herself have fun, and why she had reacted like she did when he suggested they go Christmas shopping. She blamed herself for her son's death.

She didn't feel that she deserved to be happy or that she had any right to have fun, or enjoy herself, because in her mind, she had lost that right when she left her son on that fateful day.

"You're alive, Angel. What happened was tragic, but it was an accident. No one could have prevented it, no one could have stopped it, and, Angel, no one, not even you, could have known what was going to happen. Right now, you hate Christmas because it reminds you of everything you lost, so I have a suggestion." Gabe waited a moment, until she nodded at him to continue, pleased that she seemed open to what he was about to suggest. "How about we try and make it a celebration? We can remember everything your Mum and Dad did for you when you were growing up, how much of an annoyance I'm sure your brother was." That got a smile from her. "And how much of a delight Bobby was. We don't have to make it anything big, just something small to start with, and see how that goes. Sound good?"

Gabe could tell by the look on her face that she wasn't sure. He knew he was going out on a limb here, but he realised now that, whilst he'd been doing it with the best of intentions, his previous attempts had been too much, too quickly. Baby steps is what was needed here. He needed to convince Angel that her family wouldn't want her to live her life like this, and to do that, he needed her to believe she was worthy of being happy.

"What were you thinking of doing?"
"Well, how about we put up a few photographs? Just a couple to start with, and then we can move on from there. How does that sound?"

The same look was back on her face, the one that told him she didn't want to do what he had suggested. He was half expecting her to shake her head in a defiant *'no'* gesture, but all she did was take a breath, stand, and walk over to one of the cardboard boxes that sat in the corner of the room.

After she opened it, she lifted out three frames and looked at each one. He could see her eyes were welling up again, and he got to his feet and walked over to her.

· · ·

"Are these okay?" she asked, and her voice cracked with emotion.

Gabe took one of the frames from her, seeing two people he assumed to be her parents sat at a table with a large banner behind them saying, *Happy Silver Anniversary.* Her dad wore a dark suit and red tie, which complimented the red dress his wife was wearing. They were holding hands on the table and smiling happily into the camera.

The second was a picture of two teenagers in school uniform, who were both trying to look happy but failing miserably. He recognised Angel immediately. She had hardly changed over the last few years. The boy beside her was obviously her brother, and he could tell they were twins. The resemblance between Angel and Andy was uncanny.

"We both hated that photo," Angel said. "Mum insisted on having it though."

Gabe smiled as he remembered his school photographs. His mum had bought every single one too, no matter how sleepy he looked, or how dishevelled his uniform was. *You'll look back and remember how much fun you had at school.* That's what his mum always told him, and in a way, she was right. He always smiled when he looked back through old photo albums.

When Angel handed him the third frame, she had a small smile on her face as she swiped at a tear that threatened to fall. The little boy that was grinning back at him was adorable. He was dressed in blue, from his head to his toes, and his top had a bright red slogan that said, *Mummy's Little Monster*. He still had those baby blue eyes, and he could see two small teeth as he grinned. The little boy was beautiful.

"These will be perfect."

Gabe took all three photographs and turned to look at the room. There weren't many places they could be displayed, so he walked to her bedroom and opened the door. Angel followed him and watched as he set out the three photographs on her dresser. He put the one of Bobby in the centre, with the other two flanking it. He took a step back and looked at the photos, just as Angel came to stand next to him.

They stood there for several minutes before Angel's arm went around his waist and she rested her head on his arm.

"Thank you."

Gabe could hear the emotion in her voice, so he didn't respond. All he did was wrap his arm around her shoulder and pull her into him. He held her against him as they both stood there, staring at the little boy who was no longer being hidden away and had pride of place in his mother's bedroom.

CHAPTER
SIXTEEN

ACCORDING TO GABE, she'd taken the first step. She wasn't sure she saw it that way, but she had to admit, it was nice seeing the photos of her family whenever she walked into her bedroom.

He'd told her the reason he'd put the photos in her room was because, for the time being, they were just for her. When she was ready, she could either move them into the living room, where more people could see them, or put more photos up so she had them in both rooms.

The photos had been stuck in that box ever since she'd moved into the flat eighteen months ago. She'd walked over to it hundreds of times but hadn't had the courage to open it and look inside. Something Gabe said to her had struck a chord. She'd been mourning their loss for almost three years now. She had forgotten about the life she and her family had enjoyed before she lost them.

Her mum and dad had celebrated their silver wedding anniversary six months before they died. Her brother had taken the photograph in the frame, and they each had a copy. The party they'd thrown had been a surprise, and they enjoyed every moment.

They had celebrated twenty-five years of marriage but had been together for more than thirty. Angel knew they loved each other unconditionally, and they'd had a wonderful life together. Gabe was right, they should be celebrated, and she hated to admit he'd been right.

Even though she was feeling a little better than she usually did at this time of year, she wasn't sure if she was ready to celebrate Christmas like she had done before the fire, but there was one thing she was ready for.

"So, how are we going to deal with Gemma?"

Gabe looked at her from his position leaning against the kitchen counter. If he'd been hoping she would forget about that phone call earlier, he was mistaken.

"How did she get my number, anyway?"

"I honestly have no idea," Gabe said, and she believed him.

Angel knew he didn't give it to her. He didn't even have it himself, something she needed to rectify if she was going to keep seeing him. And yes, she had finally admitted that she wanted to keep him around, at least for the time being.

"Regardless of how she got it, what do you think she's hoping to achieve?"

"I don't know that, either. You never did tell me what she said to you."

No, she hadn't, and she was hoping she wouldn't have to, but seeing as he had asked, she couldn't really *not* tell him.

"She was just trying to get a rise out of me, and I'm sad to say she got one. Normally, I wouldn't let someone push my buttons like that, but I was so surprised to receive her call, and some of the things she was saying hit a little too close to home." She put her hand up to stop him when she saw he was going to speak. "I don't want to tell you what she said, not yet anyway. I just want to figure out what to do about her, because let me tell you something, Gabe, I'm not having some little bitch tell me who I can and can't spend time with."

Gabe's eyebrows shot up into his hairline. Yeah, she had surprised herself with what she'd just said, but she'd meant every word. There was no way in hell she was going to let a woman, whom she had never met, tell her that she couldn't see Gabe. If anything, being told she couldn't see him had made her want to see him even more.

"Okay. So, what are we going to do? I've no idea why she has started causing trouble now. It's not like I've been single ever since we broke up."

"I say we just ignore her. You block her number, and I'll do the same. We just carry on as if nothing has happened, like she doesn't exist. She'll soon get bored."

Gabe gave her a look that told her he wasn't one hundred percent on board with that plan, but when he nodded in the affirmative, he took out his phone, and seconds later, told her the number was now blocked.

She nodded and stood, before walking over to where she had flung her phone earlier, pleased to see it was still in one piece. She always had been rubbish at throwing. She doubted it had actually connected with anything, just bounced a bit on the carpet. She looked up her recent calls and blocked the number Gemma had used to call her.

Angel placed her phone on the counter and shoved her hands in the back pockets of her jeans. She rocked back on her heels, and for some reason felt a little unsure of herself.

"So, what do you want to do now?"

"Well now, that's a loaded question."

The grin he gave her made her stomach do a somersault, and she knew his mind had gone straight into the gutter. Within seconds, hers was in the same place, and she realised how her question had sounded.

"I didn't mean that," Angel said as she threw a dishcloth at him, which hit him square in the face. "You said you had shopping to do. I don't think I'm ready to actually *do* any shopping, but maybe a walk around the shops could be good?"

"Yeah? You want to go to the shops?"

"I think so, yeah. Just give me five minutes to change?"

When he nodded and smiled, Angel turned and hurried to her bedroom. She leaned against the door for a moment, unable to stop the smile that crept to her lips. She really had just suggested they go and have a walk around the shops. She hadn't felt any inclination to do that in a long while. Just the thought of it used to make her want to scream and cry, but not now, and that was partly down to Gabe.

Angel crossed the room to her wardrobe and pulled out her black jeans and grey chunky sweater. She took only a few minutes to dress before she put her feet into black ankle boots. She glanced at herself briefly in the mirror, gathering her long hair into a high ponytail, then putting small silver hoops in her ears. After a quick brush of mascara on her lashes, she grabbed her bag, and she was ready.

She stepped out into the living room, seeing Gabe standing by the front door, waiting for her. Her breath hitched in her throat as she looked at him; at the way he was looking at her. No one, not even Bobby's father, had looked at her with such intensity in his gaze. It made her whole body heat up as a shiver ran through her.

"You look beautiful."

Three words. They were just three words, but they made her heart skip a beat and her pulse quicken. When he picked up her coat from the stand and held it open for her, she stepped forward and gave him her back, so he could rest it on her shoulders as she slipped her arms inside.

As she turned, he took hold of the lapels and gently tugged her forward, placing his lips against hers. He made no move to deepen the kiss, and she was about to do just that, when he pulled back.

"Thank you for trusting me, Angel. I know this isn't easy for you."

"It's easier than I thought it would be, but I think that's down to you."

Gabe smiled down at her and pulled the lapels of her coat closer together while she buttoned it up. When she had secured her bag on her shoulder, she opened the front door and they both stepped outside as she locked it. She turned back to him and he held out a hand to her, which she took without hesitation as they left the building, crossed the street to his car, and climbed inside. Within seconds, they were pulling away.

Angel had to admit she was still a little scared that she was doing this, but she had a feeling Gabe wouldn't let her fall. He'd be there, by her side, when her inevitable freak out happened, and she knew it would happen; it always did. At least this time, she wouldn't be alone.

CHAPTER
SEVENTEEN

HE COULD TELL she was nervous. Every now and then, her hand would tighten around his, and he could feel her shaking. Still, even though this was outside of the comfort zone she had created for herself, she was here, and she was doing okay.

She'd not done any shopping herself, but she had been in the shops with him, as he had needed to buy a few items. She had been unsure at first, even hesitant, but when Gabe had said they could move on if she didn't want to go inside, she had insisted they should, if he wanted to.

He held shopping bags in one hand and Angel in the other as they walked down the high street, dodging other shoppers as they went.

Angel had been quiet on the drive into town, and he had to admit, he had expected her to back out. He had detoured to his place first, so he could freshen up and change, but when they continued into town, she hadn't said anything, so they'd arrived and parked less than ten minutes after leaving his place.

She'd taken a few deep breaths before getting out the car, and while she'd been hesitant at first, she walked alongside him, making them look like any other couple out doing their Christmas shopping.

"I'm getting a little tired," she said. "How about we go find somewhere to grab something to eat?"
    "Yeah, I could eat, and I know just the place. It's only a few minutes away from here."

She smiled up at him and nodded, so he turned them off the main high street and they walked for a few minutes until Gabe stopped in front of a little pub that was tucked away at the end of the narrow street. There was no room for parking, so patrons could only get there on foot. Gabe had been coming here for as long as he could remember.

"Looks nice," Angel said as she peered at the front of the building, with its obligatory blackboard by the front door giving Christmas wishes to passers-by and patrons.
    "Glad you like it. Shall we?"
    "We shall."

Taking a step forward, Gabe pushed open the door so Angel could go ahead of him and followed her through to the main area. He smiled. It was just as he remembered it, and it always made him happy to come back here.

There were around a dozen wooden tables, each surrounded by either chairs or stools. The tables were scratched and marked, a result of being knocked and scraped over the years, but they were all clean, and, if he had to guess, had received a fresh coat of varnish. There was a dartboard on one wall, and he could hear the familiar knocking of snooker balls coming from the back room. He knew that if he went back there, he would see several older men playing cards or dominos.

He loved this place. It must have been around four months since he had last been here. Work had gotten so busy that he just hadn't had the time, so when he saw the landlady walking towards them, he was expecting an ear bashing.

"Gabriel—sorry, Gabe. It's so good to see you." Gabe bent to give the older lady a hug, then flinched when she released him and smacked his arm. "Where have you been? I've not seen you in ages."

"Sorry, Aunt Jojo, work has been crazy."

"Yes, well, I'll forgive you just this once," Jojo said, as she turned to Angel. "And who is this pretty young thing, and what is she doing with you?"

Gabe laughed, not surprised by his aunt's reaction to the pretty blonde standing next to him. She had always teased him about girls, ever since he was a teenager and started noticing them in more than just a friendly way.

· · ·

"Aunt Jojo, this is Angel. Angel, this is my aunt Joanna, Jojo for short."

"Lovely to meet you, Jojo," Angel said, and held out a hand to his aunt, a hand she quickly withdrew when Jojo pulled her in for a hug, releasing her after a few seconds.

"Oh, sweetheart, it's lovely to meet you too. It's about time Gabe found himself a nice girl." Gabe saw Angel's cheeks flush as she smiled shyly, but she didn't correct Jojo, something that pleased him more than he thought it would. "Why don't you two go and sit down and I'll bring over a couple of menus. Order whatever you want, it's on the house."

"Thanks, Aunt Jojo."

Gabe placed his hand at the small of Angel's back to guide her over to a small table in a nearby alcove. When they were both seated, he watched Angel as she removed her coat, draping it over the back of her chair as she looked around, before turning back to him.

"How did I not know this place was here?"

"It's one of those places that unless you know it exists, it's easily missed. Aunt Jojo likes it like that. She knows almost everyone that comes in here by name. She knows what they drink, and if they come in to eat, she knows what they'll order before they do."

"How long has your aunt worked here?"

"Let's see. It was originally run by my uncle. I must have been around thirteen when he took over. When my uncle passed away five years ago, my aunt took over, so she's worked here in some capacity for almost seventeen years now."

. . .

Angel nodded at his words, just as his aunt reappeared with two menus, passing one over to him and placing Angel's on the table in front of her.

"Can I get you both a drink?"

"I'll have a white wine, please," Angel said as she looked up at Jojo

"Of course, honey. Will that be a Pinot, Sauvignon or Chardonnay?"

"Pinot, please. Thank you."

Jojo smiled and nodded before looking at him. "And for you?"

"I'll just have a lemonade, please, Aunt Jojo."

"Thank you both. I'll be over in five to take your orders."

As Jojo walked off, Gabe looked at his menu, not surprised to see it hadn't changed. All the classics were on there, along with a few specials that Jojo made herself. He looked across at Angel, who was engrossed in her menu, chewing on her bottom lip.

She looked up when the bartender brought their drinks over and said her thanks before sipping the wine and returning her gaze to the menu.

Despite the rough start, today hadn't gone too badly. She'd walked around the shops with him with no real issues. Sure, she'd been a little hesitant at times, but she had sucked it up and pushed through any nerves or fear she may have felt.

· · ·

She didn't know it, but he had bought her a little present. He'd not planned on it, but he'd seen it and thought it would be perfect for her. He just hoped she liked it.

Gabe returned his attention to the menu, just as Jojo came back to their table.

"So, what can I get you?"

"I'll have the homemade steak and ale pie, please," Angel said as she put her menu back on the table.

"Sure thing, honey. Gabe, what about you?"

"The half a roasted chicken, please, Aunt Jojo."

"One steak and ale pie, and half chicken, coming right up. Say, Gabe, are you doing anything for your birthday? It's the big 3-0 this year, isn't it?"

He glanced over at Angel, who was looking at him with interest and curiosity. There was less than two weeks until the end of the year, so she must have figured out it was coming up pretty soon.

"It's your birthday? Is it soon?"

"Very soon, honey. Gabe's birthday is on Christmas Day. It was always a double celebration in our family when he was growing up."

"Really?" Angel put her elbow on the table and rested her chin on her hand. "He never mentioned it."

"Now that's a surprise. Gabe loves this time of year. He usually shouts it from the rooftops."

. . .

Gabe was willing his aunt to stop talking, seeing the look on Angel's face change as soon as she said how much Gabe loved Christmas. She was right, he did usually tell anyone who would listen that his birthday was on Christmas Day. He'd been going on about it at work for weeks, but knowing how Angel felt, he hadn't said anything.

"Usually, but Angel and I haven't known each other long, so I didn't think it was the right time."

He spoke to his aunt, but his gaze was fixed on Angel, hoping he could convey with his eyes that he hadn't meant to hide his birthday from her, and that he really was doing it so that he wouldn't upset her further.

"I guess I should get you a present then, shouldn't I?"

Gabe continued looking at her, seeing his aunt move away from the table out of the corner of his eye. The tone of Angel's voice didn't sound like she was upset. In fact, it sounded quite light-hearted.

"Why didn't you say it was your birthday soon?"
    "Well, I wasn't sure how you would react. I know you're not a fan of Christmastime, with good reason, so I didn't want to add to how you already feel, or have you feel obligated to buy me something—which you don't have to, by the way."
    "What if I want to?"
    "If you want to, I can't stop you, but don't feel like you have to."

. . .

When she folded her arms on the table and leaned forward, Gabe instinctively did the same.

"Gabe, when will you realise that I don't do anything I don't want to do."

Angel sat back and picked up her wine, taking a sip as she smiled at Gabe. He wasn't sure if there was any hidden meaning in her words, or whether he should just take them at face value, but she didn't seem to be upset that he had kept his birthday from her.

While they waited for their food, Gabe told her a little more about his family, at her request. He told her all about his older sister, Bonnie, and her three children, Felix, Maisie, and Phoebe. He adored his nieces and nephew and couldn't wait to see them on Christmas Day. Bonnie was almost ten years older than he was; the age difference being because, due to a difficult labour, his mother had been told she couldn't have more children.

She had been almost forty when she found out she was pregnant with him, and to this day she called him her 'happiest of accidents'. He was very close to his parents, who were both almost seventy.

Occasionally, Angel's face fell when he talked about his parents, but it brightened up again when he spoke of his childhood antics and the trouble he had gotten into with his sister. She might have called him a little twerp sometimes, but she'd protected him against the bullies when he'd been in secondary school. It had taken him some time to realise she was helping him and not just sticking her nose where he felt it didn't belong. She might have annoyed the hell out of him when he was younger, but he wouldn't be without her in his life.

They'd been talking for almost thirty minutes by the time their food was being brought over to them. Jojo placed two plates in front of them, pausing before she left them alone again.

"Oh, Gabe, I forgot to tell you, that girl you used to date was in here asking about you the other day."

Gabe looked at Angel, before they both turned to Jojo.

"What girl?" he asked her.
"I don't remember her name, but I think she used to have blonde hair, though it's red now. Pretty girl, but there was something about her I didn't like. I wouldn't trust that one if I were you."
"What did she say? Did you tell her anything?"
"She just asked if you had been in here recently, and where she could find you. I told her I'd not seen you in a few months, and I wasn't prepared to give her your personal information without speaking with you first. She tried it on a bit, saying how she was an old friend and she wanted to surprise you for Christmas, but as I said, there was something

about her. When I refused again, she got a little huffy and left. That was two days ago I think."

Gabe looked at Angel briefly, then turned back to his aunt.

"If she comes in again, can you tell her the same thing, but call or text me to let me know, please?"
"Sure thing, honey, but she's trouble that one. I'd steer well clear."

Jojo smiled at them both before walking back towards the bar. Gabe looked down at his food, suddenly having no appetite. Angel, however, was tucking into her pie and chips, and he threw her a puzzled look, one she picked up on when she looked up.

"What?" she asked as she swallowed a mouthful of pie.
"How can you eat right now, after what Jojo just said?"
"Simple really. We agreed to carry on as if nothing has happened, as if she doesn't exist, so that's what I'm doing. Besides, I'm starving and this food smells too good to waste."

Angel carried on eating her food as Gabe watched her. Every now and then, she would look up at him and smile, before pointing to his food with her fork. She was right. They had agreed to forget about Gemma and carry on as normal. What could be more normal than two people having dinner after a day, or rather afternoon, of Christmas shopping?

· · ·

Picking up his knife and fork, Gabe stabbed his chicken and started pulling the meat off the bone. As usual, the food was delicious, which was part of the reason people kept coming back to this place. His aunt knew how to cook and made sure everyone left with a full belly.

Fifteen minutes later, he was putting down his knife and fork and leaning back in his chair. If it wasn't for the fact he was with company, and in a public place, he'd be unbuttoning his jeans right about now. He felt as stuffed as a Christmas turkey, and he guessed Angel felt the same way as she leaned back, resting her hands on her belly.

"I don't think I can move," Angel said with a small chuckle. "Your aunt is one hell of a cook."

"Yeah, she is. She always used to cook big meals when I was younger. She's so used to cooking for lots of people, which is why her portions are so big."

"Everything okay over here?" Jojo said as she came over. "I see you're both finished."

"Wonderful as ever, Aunt Jojo. You haven't lost your touch."

"Of course not, honey. Oh, you got a phone call while you were eating. They didn't say who it was, but I have a feeling it was that girl again. I said you weren't here, so she asked me to give you a message the next time I see you. I'll admit, I'm a little confused. It doesn't make much sense to me."

Gabe was starting to get a little nervous now. He knew Gemma had been following one or both of them. She would have known about this place because she had been here when they were together, but to call and leave a message today, the same day he and Angel were there, was too much of a coincidence.

"What was the message, Aunt Jojo?"

"She said to tell you, *blondes don't always have more fun*. I told you, makes no sense."

With that, she gathered up their plates and walked away. Gabe took a breath and looked at Angel. He could tell she was shaken by Gemma's message, and as if in unison, they both stood and put on their coats. Gabe grabbed his shopping bags, rounded the table and took Angel's hand. After kissing Jojo on the cheek and saying their goodbyes, they were back out on the street, heading towards Gabe's car.

"She's just trying to spook us," Angel said as she tried to keep up with his long strides.

"Well, she's succeeding," Gabe said as they rounded a corner and moved up the street that led to the carpark. "I don't know what I ever saw in her."

"Gabe, I don't know you well, but I think I know enough about you to say if she had been like this back when you knew her, you wouldn't have been together. She's changed, Gabe. How or why, we don't know, but she isn't the same girl you knew."

Clearly, Gabe thought to himself as they neared the carpark. He had no idea why Gemma was doing this. He didn't know if she was trying to get at him, or Angel, or maybe both of them. He didn't know where she was or what she had planned, and that was the part that was scaring him.

. . .

When they got to the car, Gabe pressed the key fob and the lights flashed to indicate the car was unlocked. He dumped the bags in the boot and went around to open the passenger door for Angel. She climbed inside without a word, and when he went to walk around to his side, he saw her.

CHAPTER
EIGHTEEN

ANGEL FASTENED her seatbelt and waited for Gabe to climb in so they could be on their way. Despite her initial reservations, she was pleased she had come out today. She hadn't shopped herself, but she had been into the shops and waited while Gabe got what he needed. A week ago, she wouldn't have even done that, so she chalked it up as a huge step forward.

To top off the afternoon, she had gotten to meet Gabe's aunt. She was a woman of around sixty, if Angel had to guess, with curly brown hair that was sprinkled with grey. She wore round glasses, and Angel had noticed the sparkle in her eyes when she saw Gabe walk into her pub. There was clear love and affection there, from both of them.

After several minutes, Gabe still wasn't in the car, and she saw he was just standing in front of her, looking ahead. Taking off her belt, she opened the door, then got out, moving to stand next to him. She gently placed a hand on his back and followed his gaze, seeing a pretty redhead leaning against a car, arms folded across her chest. She looked familiar, like Angel had seen her somewhere before, and she knew instantly who it was.

"Is that her?"

She saw Gabe nod as he started forward, walking towards the other woman. Angel wanted to follow, to ask her why she was doing what she'd been doing, but she stayed where she was, knowing Gabe needed to do this on his own. But she would be there if he needed her.

To her surprise, Gemma didn't move. She'd half expected her to get in her car and drive off, but she maintained her position, even when Gabe stood right in front of her. She couldn't hear what they were saying, and part of her wished she could. Gabe's hands were on his hips, and when she unfolded her arms and reached out to him, he batted her away; a move she wasn't happy with, if her expression was anything to go by.

Angel continued watching, her body tensing when the redhead locked eyes with her from across the carpark. She shoved past Gabe and started walking in her direction, despite Gabe's shouts for her to stop. Before she knew it, Gemma was standing in front of her.

. . .

"So, you're the little bitch my Gabe is so enamoured with."

"Gemma, don't talk to her like that."

"No, it's okay, Gabe," Angel said, glancing at Gabe over her shoulder. "Let her have her say. Oh, and by the way—Gemma, is it? —he hasn't been *your* Gabe in a very long time."

"He will always be my Gabe. I was his first. He was my first. We will always mean something to each other. You will never be to Gabe what I am."

"And what would that be? The woman that killed his baby? No, you're right, Gemma, I will never be that. I *could* never be that."

Angel saw her reaction at the mention of the baby. Clearly, she hadn't thought Gabe would have revealed that piece of their history together.

"You had your chance with him, Gemma, and who knows, if you had kept the baby, you might still be together, or you might not. That's the beauty of *what ifs,* Gemma, you just never know. Gabe has moved on, so it's about time you did the same. He doesn't love you anymore. He hasn't for a long time. Do you really want to be with a man who can never forgive you? A man who looks at you and is reminded every day about what you did?"

"He will. I just need a chance to convince him. He will forgive me."

"No, Gemma. I can never forgive you for what you did."

Angel looked at Gabe as Gemma turned to him.

. . .

"You don't mean that, Gabe."

"I do, Gemma. I tried so hard to forgive you, but what you did… that's something I can never forget. If you'd discussed it with me, who knows, maybe things could have been different, but you took it upon yourself to get rid of our baby, and then kept it to yourself for weeks before telling me. Any trust I had in you evaporated that day, Gemma. I can never trust you again, and I can't forgive. You need to accept that and move on."

Gemma was crying now, and part of Angel felt sorry for her. Gabe was being as gentle but to the point as he could. He had loved this woman once, but that love had died when their baby had.

"But I love you, Gabe. I thought I was over you, but then I saw you in that bar the other night. I sang a song for you. I know you love that song. How could you not know I was singing for you? Didn't you see me? Didn't you hear me?"

Angel's eyes widened as she realised why Gemma looked so familiar. The screeching Santa from the bar. The girl on the karaoke. That had been her, and she'd been singing that song to Gabe.

"No, Gemma. I didn't see you, and I didn't hear you."

"That's her fault. It's your fault!" she said as she turned back to her, the tears still falling. "If you hadn't been there, Gabe would have seen me, and he'd have realised that it's me he wants."

"Gemma, stop it."

Gabe raised his voice, making her jump slightly. It got Gemma's attention too, as she looked at him.

"None of this is her fault. I didn't even know she existed until Friday. Everything that has happened is on you. You need to accept it and leave us alone. There's nothing between you and me anymore. There hasn't been for years, and there never will be again. Move on, Gemma, because waiting for something that will never happen is going to end up destroying you."

There was silence when Gabe finished speaking. Gemma looked between them both, before she pushed past Gabe and ran to her car. Within seconds, she was screeching out of the carpark, leaving Angel alone with Gabe.

She wasn't sure what to say to him after what had just happened, so she just turned and got back in the car. He followed after a few seconds, and they just sat there, looking straight ahead.

"So, I—"
"I want you to stay with me tonight. At my place."

Well that hadn't been what she'd expected him to say. If anything, she thought he would take her home and then go home himself. After the encounter with Gemma just now, she'd imagined he would want some time to himself, but clearly, she had been wrong.

"Um, okay. I'll need to go back to my place first though. Grab a change of clothes."

"Okay."

Gabe kept his gaze straight ahead as he drove out of the carpark and joined the traffic. He said nothing on the drive to her place and stayed in the car when she went up to get her things. When she was back in the car, he pulled away quickly, not even giving her time to fasten her seatbelt, and as soon as they were at his place, he turned off the engine and jumped out the car, leaving her to trail behind.

She figured he'd be upset after what had happened, but this ignoring her wasn't something she was happy with. Was he pissed that she had spoken with Gemma and brought up the baby? Had he wanted to deal with it on his own? Well, too bad. Gemma had dragged her into it when she'd called her, accusing her of stealing Gabe. Did he really think she was going to sit back and just let him deal with her? Not a chance in hell.

Gabe unlocked the front door and stepped inside. She followed him in, dropping her bag in the hallway before moving through the door that Gabe had just vanished through. She wanted answers, and she was going to get them.

"Look, Gabe, if you're pis—"

. . .

Those were the only words she could get out before Gabe's mouth was on hers and she was crushed between the wall and his body. It took her mere seconds to respond to his kiss as she pushed her hands into his hair, gripping the dark strands tightly as his mouth plundered hers.

When he pushed his hips forward, she felt his desire for her, and she groaned, an action he clearly approved of as his hands skimmed down her body, hooked under her thighs, and lifted her up. She was left with no choice but to wrap her legs around his waist, which only made the contact with his hardening length more intimate as she wriggled to get closer.

His mouth left hers and moved down to nibble at the pulse point on her neck, and she let her head fall back against the wall as he continued to cause wave after wave of pleasure to wash over her.

"I want you, Angel," he whispered hoarsely, his voice deeper than she had ever heard it before.

All she could manage was a weak nod, but it was all he needed to spin them around and stride across the room, his mouth still latched on to her neck as he kicked open a door. Seconds later, they were tumbling onto the bed, a tangle of arms and legs as they both fought to get closer to the other.

. . .

This wasn't how she had intended today to end, and her head was telling her to take it slow, but in that moment, Angel was listening to her body, and that was telling her to allow Gabe to take her to heaven.

And that's exactly what he did.

Twice.

CHAPTER
NINETEEN

WHEN ANGEL WOKE, it was dark. The curtains were open, and the only light in the room came from the streetlights outside. Glancing at the clock, she saw it was almost 7am on Christmas Eve, and she wasn't in her own bed.

Despite that, she wasn't ready to get up yet, so she snuggled back down into the pillows and the ridiculously warm duvet, smiling as she remembered the night before.

The things Gabe had done to her body had amazed her. He'd made it sing, and hum, and she swore she could still feel the sensations even now. Her body ached, but in a good way, and she grinned when she recalled some of the things he had said to her.

Gabe had a filthy mouth, and she found she liked it, which surprised her no end. Dirty talk had never appealed to her before, but no one had spoken to her the way Gabe had. Some of the things he said were downright indecent, and she had loved it!

Making sure the covers were over her, she turned, frowning when she noticed he wasn't lying in bed next to her. Angel pushed up to her elbows, seeing a folded piece of paper on the pillow where Gabe's head should be. Picking it up, she rolled onto her back, using the torch on her phone to create enough light so she could read it.

Angel,

Last night was A-May-Zing. You are amazing.

If you wake before I get back, I had to go to run a couple of errands, but I won't be too late. Wait for me in bed, Angel, I'll need some warming up.

Love,

Gabe

Angel read the note again and smiled, just as she heard the front door open. She quickly switched off the light on her phone and put the note back on the pillow before closing her eyes. She heard him come into the room, followed seconds later by two thuds on the floor, and a lot of rustling. Angel guessed he was removing his clothes, and she felt a cold breeze when he lifted the covers to climb in next to her.

She tried to stay as still as she could, but when he wrapped his arms and legs around her, she squealed as his cold skin came into contact with hers. Angel struggled in his hold as he chuckled behind her.

"Get off me!" she cried. "You're cold."

"Well, you'll have to warm me up, then, won't you?"

Angel struggled against him, but he was too strong, and she eventually found herself flat on her back. He had her arms pinned above her head, and her body was being pressed into the mattress by six feet plus of turned on male. When he kissed her, she forgot all about him being cold.

oOo

Two hours later, Angel was fully awake, showered, and enjoying coffee at Gabe's kitchen table. He was in his bedroom, taking a phone call from his mum, which gave her the chance to look around his place, and if she didn't already know, it was clear to anyone that Gabe loved Christmas.

There was a large real Christmas tree in the huge bay window that was easily eight feet tall. It was covered in hundreds of sparkling fairy lights with multi-coloured baubles and strands of tinsel covering it from top to bottom. The deep windowsill showed off the cards he had been sent, and all the pictures on the walls had tinsel of varying colours hanging from them.

Yes, Gabe loved Christmas, and despite recent years, Angel was finding that she didn't hate it as much as she had been trying to convince herself she should. Maybe everything Gabe had been telling her the last few days was the truth.

Angel took a sip of her coffee as Gabe walked out of his bedroom and made a beeline for where she was sat. He kissed her quickly, then moved to the counter to pour himself a cup before turning to look at her. He crossed his legs at the ankles and folded his arms, holding his coffee cup.

"So, I told my mum about you."

Angel almost spat out the mouthful of coffee she had just drunk, and just stared at him.

"Why would you do that?"

"Well, I didn't really have a choice, seeing as Aunt Jojo called her last night and filled her in on, and I quote, *the pretty blonde girl that is way out of my league.* Mum wanted to know if it was true or if Aunt Jojo was pulling her leg."

Angel wasn't sure why she was nervous. Oh yeah, that was right, she'd never been in a position where someone had told their parents about her. She didn't know how to react, or what she was meant to do.

"What did you tell her?"

"I said that it was true, and that I had met a pretty blonde girl, and yes, she is way out of my league, but it is early days, so I don't want to jinx anything."

"Okay, that doesn't sound too bad."

"Yeah, she said I should treat you well, and then said she wanted to meet you." Angel's eyes must have looked liked saucers as she listened to his words. Surely, she misheard him. "Tomorrow."

Nope, no mishearing that. Gabe's mother wanted to meet her. On Christmas Day. The one day of the year when she usually drank herself stupid and stayed in bed until it was all over.

"No, Gabe, I can't. It's way too soon."

"That's what I told her. I said we had only been seeing each other a few days, and if we were still together in the new year, I'd arrange something then, and only if you were comfortable with it."

Okay, that was better, not ideal, but better. She looked at him when he chuckled. He put his coffee down and came over to her before crouching down and taking her hand.

"If it makes you feel any better, she's looking forward to meeting you, whenever that may happen."

All Angel could do was nod as she looked down at him. She'd never met parents before. She hadn't been with Bobby's father long, and he'd wanted nothing to do with his son. She didn't even know if he had told his parents that they'd had a grandson. Even when Bobby had died, and she'd called to tell him what had happened, all she got from him was a 'sorry to hear that'. There had been no emotion whatsoever, and Angel had realised she was better off without him in her life.

"Do you want to get back to your place? I know all this Christmas stuff isn't your cup of tea."

"No, it's okay. It actually doesn't bother me like it usually does. It looks really pretty. But I think I should get back so you can finish off the shopping you didn't get to do yesterday. I have some things I need to do, too."

"Okay, I'll drop you back home. Do you want to do something tonight? Maybe a meal or a quiet night in?"

"A quiet night sounds good."

Angel smiled at him as he straightened, pulling her to a standing position.

"I'll go get my stuff together."

CHAPTER
TWENTY

GABE COULDN'T REMEMBER the last time he had felt so alive. Last night had blown his mind. The way Angel had reacted to his touch, to his words… it was like she had come alive beneath him. And he couldn't wait for it to happen again.

Right now, he was taking her back to her place, where he'd arranged a little surprise for her, one he understood was to be a massive risk. She could walk into her flat, see what he'd done, and walk straight back out to tell him she never wanted to see him again. Gabe knew that was the ultimate worst-case scenario, but he also knew that with her history, it was a very real possibility.

Her words that morning about how his Christmas decorations didn't bother her as much as they might have done before, had given him some hope. Now all he had to do was wait and see if she had meant what she had said.

He pulled up outside her place and switched off the engine.

"Can I come up? I think I left something yesterday."

Angel nodded as she got out of the car, and he breathed a

sigh of relief when she didn't ask him what he'd left there, as he wouldn't have had a clue how to respond. All he knew was he had to go up with her. He had to see her reaction when she walked in, and he hoped above all else that her reaction was a good one.

Taking a deep breath, Gabe exited the car and followed her across the street, into her building, and within moments, they were outside her front door. He watched as she pushed the key into the lock, then pushed open the door. She'd only taken two steps inside before she froze.

Gabe held his breath when she didn't say anything for what seemed like an age. When she turned to him, he saw tears in her eyes. He wasn't sure if they were tears of sadness or happiness, until she threw herself into his arms with such force he staggered backwards until he hit the wall.

It was almost ten minutes before she stopped crying. She lifted her head from his chest to look at him.

"When did you… This morning? You did all this while I was asleep?"

"Yes. I wasn't sure whether to do it or not. I almost talked myself out of it several times on the way over here. I took your keys out of your bag. I hope you don't mind?"

She smiled at him through her tears, keeping her arms around his waist as she looked over her shoulder, back into the flat. She was quiet for several minutes. All she did was hold him and look at what he'd done to her living room.

"If you had done this even as little as a week ago, I would have been so angry. Now that I know you a bit more, and after what's happened over the last few days, I can't be angry, even though there is still a small part of me that's saying I should be. I can't believe you did this for me."

"It really isn't that big of a deal. I already had the stuff, so…"

"No, it is a big deal," Angel exclaimed as she turned back

to look at him, taking his face in her hands. "Most people, when they hear what I've been through, do everything they can to stay away from me through fear of upsetting me or making me angry, but not you. You just kept showing up out of nowhere, inserting yourself into my life, even though I was a bitch to you when you first met me. I tried to push you away, even kicked you out of here twice, and you still came back. I wanted to dislike you, wanted to lump you in with everyone else who tried to tell me I should love Christmas, but no matter how hard I tried to do that—and I tried really hard—I couldn't. I guess you're here to stay, aren't you?"

Gabe listened to her words as she gently stroked the stubble on his chin. He'd been terrified that she would hate what he'd done, so the relief he felt that she appeared to be okay with it came over him in waves.

"I'm here for as long as you'll have me," Gabe said, as she smiled up at him, a fresh batch of tears filling her eyes. "Shall we go inside, so you can see everything?"

Angel nodded at him and took his hand, leading him into her flat. He closed the door and watched as she stood by her coffee table, taking in everything he had done.

After they'd placed the photographs of her family in her bedroom, he had seen she had many more stored in that cardboard box, so he had taken them out, given them a polish, and put them all out for her. Some on the walls, others on the mantelpiece over the fireplace.

On her coffee table, he had put a small two-foot Christmas tree, with a string of brightly coloured fairy lights, silver tinsel, and gold baubles of various sizes. He had strung white fairy lights around her bedroom door and along the edge of the kitchen countertops.

It had taken him about an hour to finish, and in his eyes, it wasn't much, but to Angel, he could see it meant much more.

"There's one, actually two other things," Gabe said as he

walked through to the kitchen, coming back a moment later with a bottle and two glasses. "Seeing as I won't be seeing you tomorrow, I thought we could have a little celebration ourselves. What do you say?"

He held up the bottle of champagne, seeing her face light up as she grinned and nodded at him. He popped the cork off the bottle and poured two glasses, causing her to laugh hysterically when he forgot about the fizz and one glass overflowed all over his hand. When he'd dried off, he passed one of the glasses to her, and held his aloft.

"I'd like to propose a toast. To everyone who left us too soon. You may be gone from our lives, but you will never be forgotten."

Angel gave him a watery smile before taking a sip of her champagne. He did the same before putting down his glass and walking towards the coffee table, where he picked up the small present he had placed underneath it. He handed it to Angel, who looked at it, then back at him.

"You got me a present?"

"I hadn't planned on it, seeing as we've only known each other for such a short time, but I saw them and thought they would be perfect for you."

Gabe sat on the sofa as she came to join him, peeling off the silver paper to reveal a box. The clear lid revealed four clear glass baubles. She looked at him curiously.

"You can put photographs in them. I thought you could use one for your parents, one for Andy, and another for Bobby."

"And the fourth?"

"Well, I figured if we work out, you could put one of us in that one."

He felt a little embarrassed now. He knew it was presumptuous of him to think they would be together long enough for her to want to put a photo of him in a bauble, but he would leave it up to her to decide.

"I love them," Angel said as she placed them on the coffee table and moved in to hug him. "Thank you."

Gabe held her against him and decided then and there that, even if he didn't get to see her tomorrow, this Christmas was the best one he had ever had.

EPILOGUE

Six Years Later

ANGEL SLUNG her bag over her shoulder and took a deep breath. She didn't know why she was struggling so much this year. She came here every year, did what she needed to do, said what she needed to say, and then went home, except this year there was one big difference: she wasn't alone.

She got out the car and walked to the back, opening the door for the occupant to jump out. When the car was closed and locked, she held out her hand for the little dark-haired girl to take as they stepped onto the grass and walked the short distance to their destination.

The air was crisp, and they could see their breath as they walked. Their shoes crunched in the grass, due to the ice, and she was thankful she had dressed them both for arctic weather. This was the coldest winter she could remember, and when she had checked the forecast that morning, she had been in two minds on whether or not to bring her daughter. But she had been asking about her big brother, and Angel thought it was time she got to meet him.

They reached their destination within a few minutes, and

Angel crouched down to remove some of the leaves and twigs that covered the memorial to her family. Her daughter copied her actions, and Angel had to smile at her as she watched.

The little girl was the image of her daddy. She had thick, black, curly hair, with dark eyes and a cute button nose. Every time Angel looked at her, she saw Gabe, and it always filled her heart with more love than she thought possible.

Considering how she and Gabe had met, after he had broken down her barriers against Christmas, their relationship had gone from strength to strength. There had been a few bumps in the road, one of which being Gabe's ex, Gemma.

Despite their confrontation in the carpark, Gemma hadn't left them alone, leaving she and Gabe with no option but to get a restraining order against her. The order had worked for several months, but when she started turning up at Gabe's work, he had called the police and pressed charges for harassment, stalking and breaching the restraining order. She wasn't sure what had caused it, but something had made Gemma realise what she was doing. She'd plead guilty, gotten community service, and they hadn't heard nor seen anything of her since they had walked out of the courtroom.

With the Gemma problem out of the way, they had finally been able to relax, and Angel had found out she was pregnant after they'd been together almost a year. She had freaked out at first, but Gabe had assured her he was happy, and he wasn't going anywhere. Little Eve had been born nine months later and was the apple of her daddy's eye, not to mention mummy's little princess.

The weeks and months had whizzed by, and before she knew it, she and Gabe had been together for three years. They had decided they wanted a bigger family, so they'd pooled together all their savings and had managed to buy themselves a nice little cottage on the outskirts of town, with enough land for Eve and any future children to run around.

Angel pulled a cloth and water bottle out of the bag she carried and spritzed the water over the granite, before wiping it down. She took a moment to just look at the words before reaching out to touch them as she smiled.

"Mummy, is this where Bobby is?"

"Kind of, baby."

"And Nanny and Granddad and Uncle Andy?"

"Yes, sweetie."

"So why can't I see them?"

Angel picked up her daughter and walked over to a nearby bench, sitting down with Eve on her lap.

"Do you remember what I told you, baby girl, about how they were too good for this world, so they were taken to a better place?" Eve nodded. "Well, because they are in this better place, it means we can't see them, but they can see us, and they make sure Mummy, Daddy and you are okay. Do you understand?"

"I think so. So, it's like they're invisible?"

"Kind of, yes."

"Okay, Mummy, I understand. Daddy!"

Angel released Eve as she struggled to climb off her lap. Her daughter raced off, over to where Gabe was walking towards them. She watched as he picked up their daughter and span her around, holding her in his arms as she approached her. When he came to a stop, he leaned down to kiss her, giving her a smile as he straightened.

"Daddy, did you know that Nanny, Granddad, Uncle Andy and Bobby are invisible?"

Gabe gave her a quizzical look, and Angel mouthed at him to just go with it.

"I know, poppet, they're making sure Mummy, Daddy and you are okay."

"I know, Mummy told me that already."

When she started struggling to get down, Gabe placed her on the grass and she ran over to the memorial, sitting cross-legged on the grass in front of it. Angel watched her as Gabe came to sit next to her and took her hand. They both watched their daughter talking as she waved her hands about, a trait she had picked up from Angel.

"See, I told you she would be okay."

"I know you did, but I was still worried. I almost didn't get out of the car when we arrived, but Eve asked when she was going to meet Bobby, so I didn't have a choice."

"She's smarter than she looks, that one," Gabe said as he squeezed her hand. "Mum and Dad said they've got everything set for tomorrow; they're just waiting on you to confirm what dessert you want to bring so they can coordinate the wine."

"Seriously? Why don't they just get white? It goes with everything."

"Have you met my mum? You know what she's like. If she's cooking for anyone other than her and my dad, she must have everything perfect. So, you need to text her to tell her what dessert you're taking. Oh, and I bumped into Donna on the way over here, she wants to know if you're still on for the weekend? I told her you'd text her later."

Angel nodded and took her phone out of her bag, knowing that if she didn't text Donna now, she would forget completely. Since their encounter at the ice rink six years ago, it had taken Angel a long time to realise that, while her boyfriend at the time may have pitied her, Donna didn't.

She had sought her out, knowing that she worked at a clothes shop in town, and they had slowly built the relationship she knew her brother would have wanted. They saw each other several times a month, and Donna was godmother to Eve. Andy had wanted her to be part of the family back then, and now she was.

Angel shook her head just as Eve came back to where they sat.

"I'm ready now, Mummy. I've talked to Bobby. I think we're going to be okay."

Angel smiled at her daughter and felt the tears prick at her eyes. Gabe saw them too as he leaned forward to grab Eve and swing her into the air.

"Now it's Mummy's turn to talk to Bobby, so we will go and wait in the car, where it's warm."

After giving her another kiss, Gabe strode off in the ice and wind towards the car. She waited until she heard the car doors close before she stood and walked over to the memorial.

The whole neighbourhood had chipped in so they could get this memorial. It had originally been four headstones, but everyone had clubbed together and had managed to raise close to £10,000 for the memorial for all of Angel's family.

"Hey, Bobby, it's Mummy. I hope you liked meeting Eve. She asks about you all the time. I've told her stories about you, and what you did when you were a baby. About how much you enjoyed playing with your toys. Oh god, I miss you, baby. I think of you every day, and the pain still lingers. You will always be my baby boy. I love you so much, Bobby."

Angel swiped at the tears in her eyes with one hand as she reached into her bag with the other. She pulled out an object covered in tissue paper and carefully unwrapped it. Inside was one of the glass baubles Gabe had bought her for their first Christmas. She had put a photo inside of herself, Gabe and Eve on one side, and Bobby on the other.

"I hope you like this, baby boy. I wanted to show you this because, though you might not be here anymore, you will always be part of our family." The tears started again as she crouched down, kissed her fingers, then pressed them to the photo of Bobby that had been embedded into the granite. "Love you, baby. Sleep tight."

After carefully putting the bauble back in the tissue and into her bag, Angel straightened, giving the memorial one last look before turning and walking towards the car that contained her family; the car that contained the man that had saved her life, just by approaching her in a bar six years ago.

He'd promised to make her love Christmas again, and had succeeded, which had been nothing short of a miracle. In fact, Gabe had his own name for it, a name he had come up with one night as they had lain in bed, talking about how they met. His name for what he had done?

A Winter Miracle.

ABOUT THE AUTHOR

Nicky is a British author from the West Midlands, England. When she's not writing, she loves going to the gym, musical theatre, singing, and of course, reading. She has a fondness for mint chocolate, Italian food, and a nice medium-rare steak with all the trimmings.

Follow her writing journey at:

Website: www.nickypriest.co.uk
Facebook: https://www.facebook.com/nickypriestauthor
Twitter: https://twitter.com/NickyPAuthor
Instagram: https://www.instagram.com/nickypriestauthor

Support her at:

Newsletter: https://bit.ly/3s85SZT
Patreon: https://www.patreon.com/nickypriest